Aftershock

MARK WALDEN

BLOOMSBURY

LONDON BERLIN NEW YORK SYDNEY

Bloomsbury Publishing, London, Berlin, New York and Sydney

First published in Great Britain in August 2011 by Bloomsbury Publishing Plc
36 Soho Square, London, W1D 3QY

A CIP catalogue record for this book is available from the British Library

ISBN 978 1 4088 1564 9

MIX
Paper from
responsible sources
FSC® C018072

Typeset by Hewer Text UK Ltd, Edinburgh
Printed in Great Britain by Clays Ltd, St Ives Plc, Bungay, Suffolk

1 3 5 7 9 10 8 6 4 2

www.hivehub.co.uk
www.bloomsbury.com

For Sarah
I love you

chapter one

twenty years ago

As the well-dressed old woman left the restaurant, she didn't notice that she was being watched from the dark alley across the street. The woman pulled her long coat tighter around herself and set off down the street, oblivious to the small, dishevelled figure following her. The young girl was dressed in dirty jeans and a threadbare jumper that looked several sizes too large, her long dark hair hanging down over her dirt-streaked face. She gained on the woman but was careful not to move too quickly for fear of attracting attention. As she drew closer she gave a small flick of the wrist and a knife appeared in her hand, as if from thin air. The girl increased her pace, finally breaking into a run only when she was just a couple of metres from her target. The knife flashed through the air slicing cleanly through the strap of the woman's handbag as the young girl sprinted past her, snatching the bag before it hit the ground. In the split second that it took for the woman to realise what had happened the thief was already twenty metres away.

'Hey, stop her! She's got my bag!' the woman yelled helplessly.

A man walking on the same side of the street made a grab for the girl but she evaded him by leaping on to the bonnet of a parked car and vaulting over his head in a single fluid move. The man turned and gave chase as the girl ran round the corner, weaving between pedestrians. She sprinted across the road, dodging the traffic, heading for the brightly illuminated red M sign on the other side of the street. Two policemen were standing near the entrance to the Metro, talking to a homeless man.

'Hey! Officers! That girl, she's a thief! She just stole that bag!' the man shouted, pointing at the girl.

The policemen ran to intercept her but she hurdled the railing of the stairwell leading down into the Metro station, landing gracefully on the steps five metres below. The policemen struggled past the passengers coming up the stairs. She sprinted through the underground train station, passing by the elaborate stained glass windows set into the marble walls, heading for the platforms. She leapt on to the smooth metal slope that separated the escalators and dropped on to her back, sliding down between the startled passengers and hitting the ground running. At the end of the lower concourse she stopped for a moment, listening to the sounds of the trains as the two policemen pushed their way on to the escalator. She stuffed the old woman's bag inside the waistband of her jeans and ran towards the platform on her right just as the train started to pull out of the station. She stopped running, watching as the train accelerated away from the platform, waiting for the perfect moment. Just as the policemen rounded the corner behind her she began to run again, leaping into the air at the precise instant that the last carriage whistled past in front of her. She caught the handles on either side of the door on the rear of the train and hung on as it shot into the darkened tunnel.

'Do svidaniya!' she shouted at the two astonished policemen standing on the platform as they disappeared from view.

She clung on to the back of the train as it thundered through the tunnel, waiting patiently for the light that would signal their arrival at the next stop. As they pulled into the next station and the train slowed to a halt, she hopped on to the platform and joined the crowd of people heading for the surface. She walked up the stairs leading out of the station and decided to make her way home. A few minutes later she was climbing up the fire escape on the side of a disused factory building leading to the roof. She dropped down through one of the dirty skylights and on to the floor of the long-abandoned attic that was her current bolt-hole. She headed over to a table on the far side and picked up a box of matches and lit the oil lantern that stood on it. In the small pool of yellow light she examined the contents of the stolen bag.

'How many times have I got to tell you,' a voice said from the shadows, 'you don't work on my turf.'

The girl spun round as four boys in their late teens emerged from the darkness at the other end of the room.

'What? Did you think that I wouldn't be able to find you? You thieve on my patch and I will always know where you are. Now we're going to have to teach you a lesson, you know, just to make sure that you understand the rules,' the leader said as he walked towards her.

'I'm sorry, Boris,' the girl said, as the boys moved to surround her. 'I'll give you a cut of my take. Hey, have it all if you want. I don't want any trouble.'

'Too late for that – you had your chance. In fact, I think that this time I will be the one giving you a *cut*, yes?' he said, pulling a knife from his pocket and holding it up in front of him.

One of the other boys lunged for the girl but she quickly dodged sideways and punched him in the mouth. He staggered backwards clutching at his mouth, blood oozing between his fingers. Boris watched as the other two uninjured boys ran at the girl and she dropped low, her foot lashing out at one of the boys' ankles and sending him flying. As he hit the ground with a thud the other boy grabbed the girl's arm and she spun round, driving her fist straight into his nose and knocking him backwards. She turned back towards Boris just in time to see him coming before he slammed into her and knocked her to the ground. He pinned her down and held the knife in front of her face, the reflected light from the lantern glinting in its blade.

'And now I'm going to make an example of you,' he said, bringing the tip of the knife to within a couple of milli-metres of her eye.

There were four muffled pops and a look of surprise on Boris's face as a blood-red patch began to spread across the white material of his T-shirt, directly above his heart. The girl cried out in fear as Boris's body toppled forward on to her. She pushed him off, leaping to her feet as two figures emerged from the darkness at the other end of the room. The man was tall and muscular with dark hair that was peppered with grey. He slid the silenced pistol back into the shoulder holster that he was wearing beneath his immaculately tailored suit. He had emotionless eyes which gave him a terrifying air of ruthlessness. The woman standing beside him was equally tall and strikingly beau-tiful, her long dark hair hanging straight down to her shoulders. The suit she wore was clearly just as expensive as the man's. Unlike the man, however, she was smiling. The girl backed away from them as they walked towards her, almost tripping over the body of another of the four boys that they had just murdered.

'Hello, Natalya,' the woman said, still smiling. 'I cannot tell you how glad I am to have finally found you.'

'Stay away from me,' the girl replied, still retreating. 'Stay away from me, I'm warning you.' She snatched Boris's knife from the floor. 'I mean it. I'll cut you if you come any closer.'

'No, you won't,' the man said calmly, still slowly walking towards her. 'You may try but it won't make any difference.'

The girl felt genuine fear now as she slowly stepped backwards, holding the knife defensively in front of her.

'Who are you? How do you know my name?'

'My name is Anastasia Furan and this is my brother, Pietor,' the woman replied. 'I have been searching for you for a long time, Natalya. I want you to come with us.'

'Why would I go anywhere with you? I don't even know you,' the girl replied.

'I am going to make you an offer, my dear. You can come with me now and let me try to channel your obvious talents more . . . *effectively*, or I can walk away and Pietor will shoot you and dump your body in the Moskva river,' Anastasia replied. The fact that she didn't stop smiling made the threat even more terrifying.

'So I don't really have a choice,' Natalya replied.

'You will find as you grow older that choice is rarely more than an illusion, Natalya,' Anastasia replied, holding out her hand. 'Shall we go?'

☻☻☻

The van pulled to a stop and the rear doors opened. Natalya squinted at the sudden brightness. The back of the van had no windows and during the journey the only light had been from a small grille that separated the front of the vehicle from the rear. She stepped out into the cobbled courtyard of what could only be described as a castle. The main building in front of her was surrounded by a high wall capped by battlements that were being patrolled by armed guards. At regular intervals along the walls were high towers topped by guard posts with searchlights on their roofs. Natalya had never seen anything like it before and she stood gaping for a moment before Pietor Furan motioned for her to head through the large wooden doors that led into the main building.

Inside they passed through a security checkpoint before walking into the central yard where dozens of children of all ages were sparring. They wore grey combat fatigues and black boots and were responding quickly to the barked commands of the instructors who were dotted around the area. Furan walked through the cloister surrounding the yard and led her up several flights of stairs to a door labelled 'dormitory'. She walked inside but Furan remained outside.

'Your bed and locker are at the far end,' Furan said. 'Your uniform is on the bed. Get changed and return to the combat training area.'

He closed the door behind her as Natalya walked the length of the dormitory. At the far end she found a uniform identical to the ones she had seen the other trainees wearing. She quickly slipped out of her tattered street clothes and pulled on the new uniform before heading down to the training area. There she found Pietor Furan standing in front of a group of children who all seemed to be about the same age as her. Some of them glanced at her with curiosity as she approached.

'Eyes forward,' Furan barked. 'The next hour will be spent in full-contact sparring. You will swap partners every five minutes. Any sign of hesitation or mercy for your opponent will be punished. Begin!'

The children all divided into pairs in silence as Natalya watched. A boy approached her and gave a small nod of the head before dropping into a fighting stance. Natalya barely had time to react before he launched a punishing volley of lightning fast punches and kicks, knocking her to the ground. He offered her his hand and pulled her up from the ground.

'Dimitri,' he whispered as he helped her to her feet.

'Natalya,' she whispered back. 'What is this place?'

'They call it the Glasshouse,' Dimitri said, glancing nervously towards Furan who was watching the trainees on the other side of the area. 'Attack me, quickly.'

Natalya threw a couple of weak punches at Dimitri which he blocked with fluid ease.

'What was that?' Furan snapped angrily as he marched towards them. 'Hit him!'

Natalya threw another punch, which again Dimitri blocked.

'I said hit him, not peck at him like a raven pecking at a corpse,' Furan said. 'Again!'

Natalya attacked Dimitri again, trying harder to make any of the blows count. Still she could not get through his defences.

'Still it is peck, peck, peck,' Furan yelled.

'I'm trying!' Natalya turned and yelled angrily at him.

Furan backhanded her hard across the face, knocking her to her knees. She tasted blood in her mouth.

'How dare you raise your voice to me,' he said, standing over her. 'No matter. In time you will learn some respect, my little raven, that much I can promise you.'

☙☙☙

Natalya collapsed on to her bed exhausted. The first day of training had been brutal and relentless. Her muscles were

9

sore and she knew that beneath her uniform she had to be covered in bruises.

'Sorry about earlier,' Dimitri said as he approached her bunk. 'If I'd let you hit me, Furan would have beaten the snot out of me.'

'I would love to talk but I'm afraid it makes my face hurt,' Natalya said with a pained smile.

'Don't worry,' Dimitri replied, 'it gets easier. Well, maybe not easier so much as you notice the pain less.'

'Is he always like that?' Natalya asked.

'Who? Furan?' Dimitri asked. 'Yes, I'm afraid so. You don't want to get on the wrong side of him, trust me. He's not the really scary one though. That's his sister, Anastasia. She's the one who makes my blood run cold.'

'Yes, we've met,' Natalya replied. 'And I know what you mean. So how do I get out of here?'

'What?' Dimitri asked with a frown.

'I don't know about you but I'm not planning on staying,' Natalya replied. 'So how do I get out of here?'

'Shhh,' Dimitri whispered, sitting next to her on the bunk, 'talk like that will get you killed. It's not like we don't all think about it but, if they find out you've been talking about it, you'll end up in the hole or worse.'

'So it's impossible,' Natalya said.

'I didn't say that,' Dimitri replied with a wink, 'you just have to be careful who you talk to about it.'

'Dimitri, Dimitri!' Another boy shouted, running down the dormitory towards them. 'Have you heard, there's a new girl here, she was brought in by Fur . . . oh, hello.' The boy blushed as he saw Natalya.

'And this idiot is my friend, Tolya,' Dimitri said with a lopsided smile.

'Hi, I'm the new girl,' Natalya said.

'Nice to meet you,' Tolya replied. 'Sorry, I didn't realise you were going to be in our dormitory.'

'Yes, this is my bed and if you guys don't mind I'm afraid I'm going to have to use it right now. I'm exhausted,' Natalya said.

'Of course,' Dimitri said with a smile. 'See you later, Natalya.'

Natalya gave a small wave as she rolled over in her bunk, not even bothering to put on the pyjamas that were in her locker. Within seconds she was asleep. As she slept, Natalya dreamt she was in a snow-covered field, watching Anastasia and Pietor Furan standing over her corpse and laughing as a raven fed on it. Anastasia Furan stopped laughing, turned towards Natalya and spoke.

'Peck, peck, peck, little Raven, peck, peck, peck.'

chapter two

NOW

The main hall at H.I.V.E. fell silent as Dr Nero walked across the stage to the lectern. Standing in neatly ordered rows on the polished black granite floor in front of him were the third year students of H.I.V.E. They had come from all four corners of the globe but were united by one thing. They were the children who had demonstrated a gift for the nefarious or some talent for villainy, something uniquely special that had attracted the attention of H.I.V.E., the Higher Institute of Villainous Education. They were all being trained in the art and science of villainy, being prepared, upon graduation, to take their place within the organisation known as G.L.O.V.E. The Global League of Villainous Enterprise was the most powerful clandestine group of international mega-villains that the world had ever known. The head of its ruling council, and also the headmaster of H.I.V.E., was Maximilian Nero, the very man who now stood in front of this particular group of students. He wore an immaculately tailored black suit with a white shirt and at his neck was a blood red cravat. Only the wide streaks of silver running through the jet black hair at each temple would have given an observer any hint as to his age.

'Good morning, students,' he said. 'I know that you are all busy studying for the forthcoming exams but I have gathered you here today to make a couple of important announcements. Firstly, we will soon be welcoming some new arrivals to the school. Most will be joining the lower years but a few will be joining you. These students will be unfamiliar with H.I.V.E. and will doubtless require some assistance adjusting to their new home. I know it's unusual for us to take new students into the higher years of the school like this but I will still expect you to ensure that your new classmates are given a warm welcome.'

There was a brief murmur of discussion as Nero paused and scanned the crowd.

'Secondly,' Nero continued, as the students fell silent once more, 'I wanted to inform you that the groupings will shortly be announced for the field assessment exercise or to use the more lurid nickname it seems to have attracted . . . the Hunt. For many years this exercise has been an important part of the training for every student at H.I.V.E. and I have no doubt that some of the older students will have taken great pleasure in informing you about what it entails. For those of you who do not know, the Hunt is an assessment of both your wits and your physical fitness. You will be taken to an undisclosed wilderness location and given a one hour head start before elite G.L.O.V.E. forces, led by Raven, are sent after you. Beyond that there are no rules, you must simply evade capture for as long as you possibly can. In all the years that we have been running the Hunt no one has evaded the trackers for more than twenty-four hours. That is a record I would be delighted to see beaten by somebody in this room. You have one week before the Hunt begins – further details will be sent to your Blackboxes shortly. If you have any questions please direct them to H.I.V.E.mind. Please remember that this is merely the first stage of your examinations and, while I understand that the Hunt has a certain notoriety in the school, I do not want you to focus exclusively upon it. Additional time is being allowed within your existing timetables for extra revision periods and I urge you to take full advantage of the opportunity for extra study. I will expect you all to excel in your examinations, failure will have ... consequences. Dismissed.'

Nero turned and walked off the stage as the students dispersed to their first lessons of the day amidst a buzz of excited chatter. Raven was waiting for him at the side of the stage. As usual, she was wearing a black bodysuit that was covered in pockets and pouches filled with various items of lethal equipment. Sheathed across her back, attached to her tactical harness, were the twin crossed katanas that rarely left her side. She was widely regarded as the world's deadliest assassin but, more importantly to Nero, she was also his most trusted ally.

'Natalya,' Nero said with a smile as he approached, 'is everything set for our trip to London?'

'Yes, but do I really have to wear that outfit?' Raven asked with a frown.

'You can hardly attend the opera dressed as you are, my dear,' Nero said.

'I suppose. Did Wright tell you what it is that he wants to discuss?'

'No, but I can make an educated guess,' Nero said with a slight sigh. 'I know this meeting may be pointless but Joseph served G.L.O.V.E. loyally for many years. I should at least hear what he has to say. I owe him that much.'

'It could be a trap,' Raven said.

'Which is why I'm bringing you along,' Nero said with a smile. 'Besides, I haven't seen *Don Giovanni* in years.'

☮☮☮

'As if we don't have enough to worry about with the exams,' Otto said with a sigh as he walked along the corridor leading to the Villainy Studies department with Wing and Shelby.

'Now we have to go and play hide and seek with Raven in some godforsaken corner of the planet as well.'

'I think it might actually be quite fun,' Shelby said happily, 'and I don't know why you're getting so worried about the exams, computer brain. Can't you just, I don't know, download the entire library or something?'

Otto did, in fact, have something of an unfair advantage over his friends when it came to studying. He had, after all, been genetically engineered from birth to act as a physical host to an insane artificial intelligence. Thankfully, since the final destruction of Overlord several months earlier, he no longer had to worry about that horrific possibility but he still carried the hardware around inside his skull that would have made it possible. The organic super computer implanted in the centre of his brain made him capable of near instantaneous comprehension and perfect recall. It was something which he had always taken for granted and he sometimes forgot that his friends probably still found it slightly odd.

'I'd happily swap all the suffering that this thing in my head has caused for having to do a bit of revision, believe me,' Otto said with a sad smile.

'We all know that, my friend,' Wing said, putting his hand on Otto's shoulder. 'None of what happened with Overlord was your fault.' Their final encounter with the psychotic artificial intelligence had cost the life of their friend and fellow Alpha student, Lucy Dexter, a loss which they all still felt acutely. 'I must admit though that I too, like Shelby, find the prospect of this Hunt intriguing.'

'Yeah, well, it's all well and good for you wannabe ninjas,' Otto said with a smile. 'Some of us actually don't find the idea of being chased through the wilderness by Raven and a bunch of G.L.O.V.E. goons particularly exciting.'

'That's OK, you can act as a diversion,' Shelby grinned. 'The ten minutes that it takes Raven to catch you will be ten minutes she's not searching for me. I want that twenty-four hour record and every little helps.'

'And the selfless spirit of teamwork continues to burn brightly at H.I.V.E.,' Otto said. 'You know, it's actually quite moving.'

'Hey,' Shelby said, 'it's not my fault you're the slowest zebra.'

'Speaking of helpless prey . . .' Wing said as they rounded the corner leading to the classroom. At the far end of the corridor Laura was walking out of an office with her head bowed as a woman in an orange jumpsuit handed her Blackbox back to her. The woman was Chief Dekker, H.I.V.E.'s new head of Security and someone who was rapidly becoming a major headache. She was tall and pain-fully thin with short grey hair and eyes that always seemed somehow to be watching you. She had been appointed after the untimely demise of H.I.V.E.'s former head of Security,

17

Chief Lewis, and she had been a thorn in their sides ever since her arrival at the school. She had made it abundantly clear that Otto and his friends were right at the top of her to-do list and that was proving to be a rather unpleasant place in which to find oneself. She scowled at the Alphas before closing the door to her office as Laura walked towards them, looking shell-shocked.

'What did the Wicked Witch of the West want this time then?' Shelby asked as Laura approached.

'Oh, just the usual,' Laura replied, sounding rather shaken. 'Where have I been, where am I going, let's just check that on your Blackbox, shall we? You know.'

'Geez, what's her problem with us exactly?' Shelby said, sounding angry. 'It's not like we've done anything to deserve this . . . well, not done anything recently at any rate.'

'She does seem to rather have it in for us. I can't imagine why,' Otto said.

'I suspect that it may have something to do with the fact that we have been directly involved with the near destruction of H.I.V.E. on at least four separate occasions,' Wing said matter of factly.

'Yeah, I suppose that might have *something* to do with it,' Otto replied with a crooked smile.

Otto lay on his bed in the quarters that he shared with Wing reading a book called *International Banking: Supervillainy for the Twenty-First Century*. To a casual observer it would have looked like he was just searching for a certain place in the book as he flicked through it, turning the pages at the rate of two per second. The strange truth was that he was actually reading. It was just one more side effect of the unusual abilities that he been born, or, more accurately, *engineered* with. Wing, meanwhile, was sat at his desk, looking slightly frustrated as he studied his notes from one of their recent Science and Technology lessons.

'Anything I can help with?' Otto asked, noticing the look on his friend's face.

'I am finding the mathematics of atmospheric re-entry rather perplexing,' Wing replied with a sigh.

'I told you,' Otto replied, 'just start with the simple stuff, Newton's laws of motion and universal gravitation and its application to orbital dynamics.'

'Oh yes,' Wing replied, rolling his eyes, 'the simple stuff.'

'Want a hand?' Otto asked again.

'No,' Wing replied firmly, shaking his head. 'You will not be able to help me in the exams. I must try to understand this for myself.'

'OK, let me know if you change your mind,' Otto said. He was just starting to feel slightly guilty as the exams approached. He might find them trivially easy, but he knew that all of his friends were getting extremely stressed at the prospect of the looming tests. There was a beep from the door and Wing got up and pressed the unlock button beside it.

'Hi, guys,' Laura said. 'You busy?'

'Hey,' Shelby said, striding past her, 'they're never too busy for us, right?'

'Our lives wouldn't be complete without you,' Wing said with a wry smile.

'Awww, you're so cute,' Shelby said, giving him a peck on the cheek.

'What's up?' Otto asked as Laura walked inside and closed the door behind her.

'Well, I've had an idea but it's something that I'd need some help with so I just wanted to run it past you guys and see what you thought,' Laura said.

'Sure,' Otto replied. 'What have you got in mind?'

'Well, just like the rest of you, I'm getting really sick of the hard time we're all getting from Chief Dekker at the moment and I reckon that it's time we took her down a peg or two.'

'Go on,' Otto said, putting down his book and leaning forward, suddenly interested.

'So I was thinking about the fact that she's been put in charge of security for the exams and it struck me how it might be really, really embarrassing for her if someone was to, I dunno, *borrow* the exam questions.'

'Laura Brand, that is one of the most dishonest and devious things you have ever suggested,' Otto said. 'I love it!'

'That's what *I* said,' Shelby grinned.

'Hmmm,' Wing said with a slight frown. 'Wouldn't that be cheating?'

'It's called securing a tactical advantage,' Otto replied quickly. 'With the added bonus of rubbing Dekker's nose in it. Only problem with that is the exam papers are stored in H.I.V.E.mind's core memory which is the most secure data storage in the school.'

'How do you know that's where they are?' Shelby asked.

'Well,' Otto replied, looking slightly shifty, 'I might have already . . . erm . . . considered this possibility myself and made some very gentle probes of the network to see if I could find the exam papers, you know, lying around anywhere.'

'I am surrounded by dishonourable people,' Wing said with a sigh.

'Hey, honeycheeks, this is the Higher Institute of *Villainous* Education,' Shelby said. 'That's kinda the point.'

'The problem is that ever since I had H.I.V.E.mind as a passenger up here,' Otto tapped the side of his head, 'I can't access anything other than the school's most basic network layer without old wireframe-head knowing. I have no idea how we'd get access to his core memory without him noticing. I even tried just asking him for the exam papers because he still owes me for letting him ride around inside my head a few months back. He told me that even if he wanted to he couldn't. He's under direct command from Nero to keep the examination papers secure within his own core memory. I doubt it's a coincidence that's the one place that Nero knows there's no way I can get at them.'

'I might have a way round that,' Laura said with a smile, 'but we're going to need some equipment that could be difficult for us to get our hands on and at least two more people to help out.'

'If only we knew someone who specialised in procuring hard to obtain items,' Shelby said with a grin. 'Come on, tell Aunty Shelby. What do you need?'

☻ ☻ ☻

Dr Nero did not turn as the door to the private box opened behind him. He did not really want to be distracted from the final moments of his favourite opera. There was something that appealed to Nero about Don Giovanni's shameless refusal to repent his wicked ways as he was finally dragged down to the underworld. When the time came, Nero imagined that he would probably feel just the same way.

Joseph Wright, the former head of G.L.O.V.E.'s British operations, sat down in the seat next to Nero's.

'I'm sorry I could not get here earlier – something came up,' Wright said quietly. 'I hear that this new baritone is quite talented.'

'Indeed,' Nero replied, not taking his eyes off the stage. 'What can I do for you, Joseph? While I must admit that spending an evening in London is always a pleasure, I got the impression from your message that you had something rather urgent to discuss.'

'Yes, of course,' Wright replied. 'I wanted to see if I could make one last attempt to persuade you to stop this madness and reinstate the former members of the ruling council while there is still time. I understand that the events of the past few months have been difficult for you, as they have been for all of us, but I still believe that there has to be another way.'

'If that is all you brought me here to discuss then I fear we have both made a wasted journey,' Nero replied. 'My decision to disband the council was final. I have no intention of changing my mind.'

'Please, Max, listen to reason. Do you really believe that all of the members of the council are simply going to walk away from their former lives? They have too much invested in G.L.O.V.E. for that. They're angry, Max, and they're not, generally speaking, the sort of people who try to resolve their problems peacefully.'

'I am quite aware of the way in which my former colleagues usually deal with these situations,' Nero replied, 'and that is part of the reason that I have replaced them. The ruling council was designed to act as a mechanism to control the worst impulses of our villainous brothers and sisters and in that it largely succeeded, but we both know that G.L.O.V.E. was dying. We had become too set in our ways, too comfortable with our power. We were blind to what was happening around us as Overlord and his Disciples rose to power and it very nearly cost the lives of every human being on this planet. G.L.O.V.E. had to change: it needed new blood, new leaders who would understand the dangers of such complacency.'

'With you in charge,' Wright said, a slightly bitter note in his voice. 'That's very noble of you, Max.'

'For now,' Nero replied, still watching the concluding ensemble of the opera. 'But I have no desire to stay as the head of the council for any longer than is absolutely necessary. As soon as the new members of the council have a little more experience and I have identified which of them would be best suited to replace me I will step down. I do have a school to run after all.'

'A school that trained every single member of the new ruling council. Do you understand what that looks like to the people they replaced? Try to look at it from their perspective.'

'What are you asking me for, Joseph, an apology? For me to change my mind?' Nero asked, turning and looking Wright in the eye for the first time.

'No, I know you too well for that, Max. I just hoped that I could make you see sense before this situation gets any worse. I can see now that I was wasting my time.' He stood up to leave. 'Goodbye, Max.'

Nero sat in silence as the opera finished, applauding as the cast took their final bow. He had suspected that this was what Wright had wanted to discuss with him and he was quite aware of the events his refusal to change his mind may set in motion. In some ways it was inevitable but it did not make the prospect of open conflict between G.L.O.V.E. and the former members of its own ruling council any more pleasant.

He made his way down from the private box and through the foyer of the Opera House before stepping out into the cool night air of Covent Garden. As usual in London the streets were still busy even at this late hour.

'I wish you'd let me sit in the box with you,' Raven said as she came and stood beside him. She was wearing a stunning black cocktail dress, as different as one could imagine from her usual uniform.

'I appreciate your concern,' Nero replied with a slight smile, 'but I think that might have made Joseph rather nervous.'

'Good,' Raven replied with a frown, 'he should be nervous. He practically threatened you in there.'

'We knew it might come to this, Natalya,' Nero replied as a black executive saloon car pulled up to the kerb. 'Now we just have to wait and see what they do next.' Nero ushered Raven to the waiting car and they both climbed inside.

'Take us to the rendezvous point,' Nero instructed the driver. There a Shroud, one of H.I.V.E.'s stealth dropships, was waiting to transport them back to the school.

'Do you really think it's wise for us to wait for them to make the first move?' Raven asked as the car made its way through the busy streets.

'I will not be the one to declare war,' Nero said, shaking his head. 'Perhaps conflict is inevitable but I won't be the one that starts it.'

'It could make us look weak,' Raven said.

'Let them make their move and then they will see how weak we are,' Nero replied.

Raven recognised the steely determination in Nero's voice, the very same determination that had propelled him to the head of the most powerful criminal organisation on Earth and then kept him there.

'Why are we slowing down?' Raven asked the driver as she felt the car suddenly decelerating.

'Road's blocked, Miss,' the driver said, pointing to the road ahead where a lorry was unloading cardboard boxes on to the pavement. Raven stared at the men unloading the lorry and felt the hairs on the back of her neck stand up as one of them glanced at their car for just a moment too long.

'Get us out of here!' Raven snapped.

The driver hesitated for a moment and then saw Raven's expression. He threw the car into reverse and hit the accelerator just as two high-sided vans pulled into the road behind them, blocking them in. The doors in the side of the vans slid open and half a dozen men in black body armour leapt out raising assault rifles.

'Get down!' Raven yelled as the soldiers behind them opened fire. The car rattled and shook as the high velocity rounds struck it. The car was armoured, of course, but there was still a limit to how much damage it could take before it was disabled. The driver threw the car into a forward gear and floored the accelerator, aiming for the narrow gap between the lorry ahead of them and the parked cars that lined the streets on either side. Raven saw one of the men reach into a box on the pavement. He pulled out a long tube-shaped object, placing it on his shoulder as he turned towards their speeding vehicle. There was a bright flare from the rear end of the tube and a missile shot down the street and struck the front of the car. The explosion flipped the car over and it landed with a sickening crunch on its roof, sliding to a halt thirty metres further down the road, its whole front end now little more than a twisted shell of burning metal.

The gunmen from the two vans walked slowly towards the burning remains of the vehicle. The point man signalled for the other soldiers to spread out around the car as he approached the passenger door. He knelt down and carefully peered inside. He immediately saw that the passenger compartment was empty and the door on the other side was ajar. There was the sudden clinking sound of something metal hitting the road behind him and he spun round just as the flashbang stun grenade detonated. He dropped to one knee, trying to regain his composure as bright swirling blobs of colour filled his vision, his retinas temporarily overloaded by the overwhelmingly bright flash from the explosion. At first there was nothing but ringing in his ears but that slowly cleared, replaced by startled screams and snapped bursts of what sounded like uncontrolled panic fire from his own team. He rubbed his eyes as things slowly came back into focus. A blurry figure strode towards him holding a pair of long, thin objects glowing with purple light.

'Such a shame, I was starting to really like this dress,' a woman's voice with a Russian accent said, still muffled slightly by the ringing in his ears. Then there was a flash of purple and everything went black.

Raven stepped back as the last member of the assault team toppled forward on to the road in a pool of his own blood. She glanced up the road towards the men around the lorry and saw that they were pulling more weapons from the boxes on the pavement. She ducked behind the still burning wreck of their car and dashed between the parked cars at the side of the road. Nero, who Raven had dragged from the burning wreckage, was unsteadily getting to his feet, an angry expression on his face.

'The driver?' he asked and Raven simply shook her head.

'Time to go,' she said, pulling the sheaths for her katanas from the back of the ruined car and strapping them on to her back.

'Do you actually go anywhere without those?' Nero asked, gesturing to the glowing purple blades of Raven's modified swords.

'I didn't wear them to the opera, if that's what you're asking,' Raven replied, looking down the street towards the men from the lorry who were cautiously advancing towards the burning car, weapons raised. 'I left them in the car. I thought they might draw a little too much attention.'

'It is a shame about your dress,' Nero said as they hurried down the pavement away from the advancing assassins, using the parked cars for cover. Raven's dress was scorched and torn in several places.

'You can buy me another one when we get out of here,' Raven replied as she glanced towards the far end of the road where she could see flashing blue lights. 'Hold these.' She handed Nero her swords.

The policeman was just climbing off his motorbike as Raven ran towards him.

'Oh, officer, please help,' she said in a frightened voice as she approached him. 'There's been a terrible accident.'

'It's OK, miss,' the officer said. 'Just calm down and try to tell me exactly what happened. Ambulances are on the w—'

He would later tell his colleagues that he had no memory of how he had been knocked unconscious. It was less embarrassing than admitting he'd been sucker punched by a beautiful Russian woman in a cocktail dress.

'Get on,' Raven said, taking her swords back from Nero and strapping them to her back before climbing on to the unconscious policeman's motorbike. 'And signal the Shroud.'

'You are aware, of course, that I hate motorbikes,' Nero said with a sigh as he climbed on to the back of the bike. He reached into his inside pocket as Raven started the bike and hit the emergency signal on his Blackbox. Raven gunned the engine and the bike shot away down the road.

'This is not dramatically improving my opinion of motorbikes!' Nero yelled from behind her as she wove at high speed through the slow-moving traffic ahead of them.

Raven glanced at the rear-view mirror and caught a glimpse of something moving more quickly through the traffic. There were three motorbikes behind them, each with a passenger riding pillion. Raven knew that they had to be the backup team that would be sent after them if they had somehow escaped the roadblock. She knew this because it was exactly what she would have done.

'We've got company!' she yelled to Nero, who twisted round and looked behind them.

'Friends of yours?' Nero replied.

'Yeah,' Raven said with a grim smile, 'I think they're just trying to return some bullets they borrowed from me . . . at about nine hundred and fifty metres per second.'

Raven jammed the throttle open, suddenly grateful for the big engine in the police bike. She roared up the on-ramp leading up to one of the elevated stretches of high speed dual carriageway that crossed central London. The traffic was not really any lighter up on this new road but it was at least moving more quickly. Raven glanced in the rear-view mirror again and saw that their pursuers were still gaining on them despite the fact she was at full throttle. There was a muzzle flash in the rear-view mirror and a split second later the same mirror exploded into a thousand pieces as it was struck by one of the bullets that whistled past them. Raven weaved left and then right, trying desperately to make them as difficult a target as possible. Despite their situation, she almost laughed out loud as she caught a fleeting glimpse of the astonished look on the face of a passenger in one of the cars they screamed past. Anybody would have thought they'd never seen a woman in a cocktail dress and a man in a dinner suit on the back of a stolen police motorbike.

She knew that they were running out of time. The bikes behind them were gaining and it would only take one bullet to end this chase very abruptly. She kept sweeping left and right across the road as another bullet pinged off the bodywork at the rear of the bike.

Suddenly a portal appeared to open in the sky about fifty metres ahead of them as the rear hatch of the cloaked Shroud dropship that had been summoned by Nero's emergency signal slid open. The pilot was trying to stay at the same speed as their bike but the loading ramp leading up into the aircraft's interior was still a couple of metres off the ground. Raven knew that if the Shroud flew any lower it would risk a collision with one of the vehicles on the road ahead. She accelerated, closing the distance to the open hatch, her mind racing. How were she and Nero going to both get on board? A crazy idea flew through her mind and in the same instant she realised that it might be their only chance.

'Get me the pilot of that thing on your Blackbox,' Raven yelled to Nero. After a couple of seconds he passed her the slim device. Raven quickly shouted instructions to the pilot before handing the PDA back to Nero. She pulled one of the swords from her back and set the control on its hilt to switch the variable geometry forcefield that ran along its edge to its sharpest setting. Raven swerved the bike left, towards the safety rail that ran along the side of the raised carriageway as yet another volley of bullets chewed up the tarmac where the bike had been just a split second earlier. She held out the glowing blade and braced herself as its mono-molecular edge sliced through the steel uprights that held the safety rail in place. The blade passed through support after support, each one giving way with a small shower of sparks. After a few seconds she kicked out and sent ten metres of the unsupported safety barrier tumbling over the side of the road.

'Keep your head down,' Raven yelled to Nero as she braked hard and spun the bike round to face the direction they had just come from, leaving a smouldering semicircle of black tyre rubber on the road. 'This could get a little bumpy.'

The bikes that had been chasing them were now only a hundred metres away as Raven gunned the engine and sent the police bike shooting back down the dual carriageway, straight towards them. Raven swerved hard to the right as a bullet passed by her head so close that she heard it buzzing like an angry hornet. She aimed the bike straight for the gap she had just carved out of the safety barrier and held her breath. As the front wheel of the speeding bike passed over the edge of the tarmac the dimly illuminated interior of the Shroud rose into view and the bike vaulted the gap. After what seemed like an interminably long second hanging in the air, the bike's front wheel slammed down on the drop-ship's loading ramp as Raven jammed the brakes on hard, ditching the bike on its side and pushing her and Nero away from it. The pair of them slid to a halt as the bike cartwheeled through the Shroud's cargo bay before slamming into the bulkhead at the far end with a metallic crunch.

'GO!' Raven yelled towards the cockpit, leaping to her feet and slapping the button that closed the rear hatch. She ducked down as the pillion gunmen on the two bikes on the road below opened fire. They were wasting their time. The Shroud was too well armoured to be taken down by small arms fire. The hatch closed with a clunk and Raven braced herself as she felt the Shroud's huge turbine engines rotate from their vertical hover position to full forward thrust as the invisible aircraft rocketed up into the night sky. Nero slowly sat up and brushed himself down.

'Not a typical trip home from the opera,' he said with a wry smile.

'Are you OK?' Raven asked.

'A few bruises in the morning I should imagine,' Nero replied, getting slowly to his feet. 'But other than that I'm fine.'

'Good,' Raven replied. 'I think we both know what that was.'

'Indeed,' Nero said with a frown. 'It appears that the time for discussion has passed. If it's a fight that our former allies want then that, my dear, is exactly what we are going to give them.'

chapter three

'I still think it would be easier to just revise for our examinations,' Wing said with a sigh.

'And again he misses the point,' Shelby said, grinning.

They sat on the bed in Otto and Wing's room in accommodation block seven and watched as Laura and Otto worked carefully on the dismantled device on the desk opposite.

'It's not cheating,' Laura said defensively. 'It's about seeing whether or not it can be done. It's the intellectual challenge of it.'

'And the cheating,' Otto said quickly, 'don't forget the cheating.'

'Hmmm,' Wing said with a look of obvious disapproval on his face.

'You're not helping, you know,' Laura said, elbowing Otto in the ribs.

'What?' Otto said as he finished soldering one of the contact points on the device in front of him. 'It's not like we're being trained to follow the rules here. If anything, I think Nero should reward us for our determination and initiative.'

'Can you fit "determination and initiative" on a headstone?' Laura asked as she leant in to examine Otto's handiwork.

'Now who's not helping?' Otto said as she peered through the magnifying lens at the device.

'Looks good,' Laura said. 'We'll make a hacker out of you yet, Malpense.'

'Stop, you're going to make me blush,' Otto said with a grin.

'All done then?' Shelby asked, standing up and walking over to Laura and Otto. 'Because you know how much I enjoy sitting and listening to you two rattle on about quantum phase discombobulators and all, but I'm exhausted.'

'Do we really need to stop now?' Laura asked. 'What time is it?'

'Ten minutes till lockdown,' Shelby replied glancing at her Blackbox PDA, 'and I for one do not want to end up being escorted to my room by security.'

'Yeah, let's just try and stay underneath Dekker's radar as much as possible for the moment, shall we? I doubt that she'd be happy to find out what we've been working on,' Otto said as he opened one of the desk drawers and lifted out the false bottom that he had recently installed. He placed the device inside the hidden compartment along with the various tools that they had managed to acquire from around the school.

'You are, of course, assuming she doesn't already know,' Wing said with a slight frown.

'Hey, look on the bright side, big guy,' Shelby said, quickly kissing him on the cheek, 'if she does know, at least we'd be locked up together.'

'Hmmm,' Wing replied, still frowning.

'Come on, Shel,' Laura said, trying hard not to laugh at the expression on Wing's face. 'Let's leave these two to get their beauty sleep. Heaven knows they need it.'

'Funny,' Otto replied. 'No really, you're funny. Look at me laughing.'

'Awww, did she hurt your feelings?' Shelby said as Laura walked out of the boys' room. 'Don't worry, we love you really. Even with that face.'

'Missing you already,' Otto said as Shelby hurried after Laura. 'Or it might just be stomach cramps, it's hard to tell, to be honest.'

Otto put the rest of the contents of the desk drawer back in place, making sure that the hidden compartment was properly concealed.

'Are you sure that this is wise?' Wing asked, gesturing towards the drawer. 'Especially if Chief Dekker is watching us as closely as you believe she is.'

'Probably not,' Otto replied, 'but let's face it, it's hardly the first time that we've done something that was a bit risky.'

'I suppose,' Wing replied, 'but I have actually been quite enjoying the fact that the past few months have had a lower than average amount of mortal peril. Indeed, I am almost at the point where I have forgotten what it is like to be afraid for my life or those of the people I care about.'

'Don't worry,' Otto replied with a smile. 'I'm sure that something spectacularly dangerous will happen soon enough. We wouldn't want life to get boring, now would we?'

'I like boring,' Wing said, raising an eyebrow. 'In fact, I would go so far as to say that I am becoming a genuine fan of boring.'

'I'll be sure to let Shelby know just how boring you think the past few months have been,' Otto said, grinning. 'I'm sure she won't mind.' Otto never liked to miss a chance to tease his best friend about his relationship with Shelby and this was too good an opportunity to pass up.

'I'd rather you didn't,' Wing said, the tiniest smile appearing on his face. 'I am still training her in the art of self-defence and our sparring sessions are quite painful enough as it is, thank you.'

'You guys are still getting on OK, I assume?' Otto asked as he pulled his Blackbox out of his pocket and placed it on his bedside table.

'Yes, though it is occasionally puzzling,' Wing said with a slight frown. 'It sometimes appears that what Shelby says she wants and what she actually wants are two entirely different things. It can sometimes lead to . . . confusion.'

'I really hate to tell you this, Wing,' Otto said with a grin, 'but I think that's actually the way it's supposed to work.'

☻☻☻

Dr Nero looked up from the tablet display he had been studying as Raven walked into his office. He nodded towards the seat on the other side of his desk.

'I've received word from other members of the new ruling council,' Nero said as Raven sat down. 'There were assassination attempts on several of them at exactly the time that we were attacked in London. Two were successful. Jacobs and Milton are dead.'

'Damn it,' Raven said softly. 'Why did we not see this coming?'

'To be honest, I did,' Nero replied, 'but there was still a part of me that was hoping it would not come to this. The former council members may not be a part of G.L.O.V.E. any longer but they still have considerable resources at their disposal and they are of course intimately familiar with the way in which our organisation operates. They will have operatives within G.L.O.V.E. who are still loyal to them and I would expect them to ruthlessly exploit any weakness that those informants expose. There could hardly be a more dangerous enemy.'

'I could try to root out any traitors who are feeding them information,' Raven suggested.

'No,' Nero replied, 'the last thing we need just now is a witch hunt. That's exactly what they want, us turning inwards and fighting amongst ourselves. We just need to be doubly cautious and ensure that we control precisely who has access to sensitive information at the moment. Speaking of which, I've just been reviewing the dossiers of the latest intake of students.' Some of them have great potential.'

'You still want to go ahead with the retrieval of the new intake under the circumstances?' Raven asked.

'Yes,' Nero replied. 'I will not let this disrupt the normal running of H.I.V.E. The new intake proceeds as planned.'

'Understood. The retrieval teams are all on standby,' Raven answered with a nod. 'Just give the word and we can begin the operation.'

'Good,' Nero said. 'I trust that you don't foresee any particular problems.'

'No, a couple of the targets have proven to be somewhat . . . elusive, but it's nothing I can't handle.'

'Of course,' Nero replied. He had learnt over the years that there were very few problems that the woman sat opposite him could not resolve. 'And preparations for the Hunt?'

'Everything's in place,' Raven said with a slight smile. 'I've reconnoitred the operational area and it's all clear. I'll be ready to run the first assessment exercise as soon as the new student recruitment is complete. You know, in a strange way I'm actually quite looking forward to spending some time in that part of the world. It's really quite beautiful, you know. It will almost be like a holiday.'

'Remind me to never let you select my vacation destinations,' Nero replied.

'If I didn't know better, I'd say you were getting soft, Max,' Raven said with a wry smile. 'You should come along and monitor the Hunt in person. Get out from behind that desk for a while.'

'I'm quite happy behind this desk, thank you,' Nero replied, raising an eyebrow slightly. 'And I'll be perfectly content to track the progress of the Hunt from a secure and more importantly *warm* monitoring station.'

'Definitely getting soft,' Raven said, her grin widening as she stood up to leave. 'So, do you want me to launch the retrieval operations?'

'Yes, but make sure that the catch squads understand the need for caution at the moment, Natalya,' Nero said. 'There are quite enough ruffled feathers out there already without us adding any more fuel to the fire.'

Nero was particularly keen to make sure that the operation to forcibly recruit the latest crop of students for H.I.V.E. went smoothly. The school needed new blood now more than ever. Events surrounding the demise of Overlord had led to him taking the highly controversial decision to disband the ruling council of G.L.O.V.E., the Global League of Villainous Enterprise. To say that decision had caused chaos amongst the ranks of the world's villains was an understatement. A few of the members of the council had agreed with his reasoning and were cooperating with his plan to rebuild G.L.O.V.E. as a more stable organisation, without the treachery and deceit that had run like a cancer through the old league. Most, however, had argued that what he was attempting was little more than a massive *coup d'état* and that he was simply trying to consolidate his own power base. He had to concede that he could understand why some people would see it that way. He may have known that his motives were genuine but it had proven impossible to convince many of G.L.O.V.E.'s former leaders that that was the case. One of the side effects of all of this was that H.I.V.E. had lost a significant number of students. While many of the children at the school were recruited against their will after displaying some particular talent for villainy, some were what Nero referred to as legacy students. They were the students whose parents were already part of the global villain community and had elected to send their offspring to H.I.V.E. so that they could be prepared for entry into the family business. A significant number of those students had been withdrawn from the school in protest at Nero's decision to disband the council. The last thing he needed at the moment were any further complications.

'Trust me,' Raven replied, 'no one will ever know we were there.'

☢ ☢ ☢

'Observe!' Professor Pike yelled over the high-pitched whine from the generator. 'The beam is quite capable of cutting through a foot of stainless steel and yet the refractive coating on this backplate renders it completely harmless. This allows friendly units to be protected against the effects of the weapon without requiring heavy armour plating.'

The bright green beam from the massive projector at the far end of the Science and Technology department laboratory lit the entire room with an eerie glow. The Alpha students who were watching the demonstration stood with their backs pressed against the opposite wall, as far away from the device as humanly possible. They had learnt from bitter, often painful, experience that it was never wise to stand too close to one of Professor Pike's experimental devices. Waiting for eyebrows to grow back was an inconvenience but waiting for limbs to grow back was another matter altogether.

'Once in orbit, the weapon can be used for precise strikes on specific targets,' the Professor continued, 'minimising the need for messy collateral damage. Mr Argentblum, would you be so kind as to dim the lights please so that I can demonstrate the importance of a precise refraction index.'

Franz nervously slid along the wall towards the light switch by the laboratory door. He flicked the switch and the room darkened, the powerful beam of laser light now providing the only illumination. Franz started to slide back along the wall towards the other Alpha students. Suddenly he felt his foot catch on something and he stumbled over one of the trailing cables that lay across the laboratory floor. The cable went tight and pulled one of the instruments monitoring the beam over, sending it falling sideways and knocking the edge of the frame that held the refractive shielding plate in position. For what seemed like a very long time the stand wobbled back and forth before it tipped slowly backwards with a crash.

'Take cover!' Professor Pike screamed, diving behind one of the nearby workbenches as the other Alpha students scattered, trying to shield themselves behind the most solid objects they could find. The beam punched straight through the laboratory wall in a cloud of vapour and alarm klaxons started wailing all over the school. Professor Pike scrambled across the floor towards the bundle of thick power cables that led to the super-laser, pulling them from the back of the machine and extinguishing the bright green beam.

'Oops,' Franz said as the emergency lighting kicked in and the rest of the Alphas slowly emerged from their hiding places. At the back of the room there was a perfectly circular, twenty-centimetre hole in the wall surrounded by scorch marks. 'I am thinking that this is not being good.'

Otto walked cautiously up to the smouldering hole, glancing nervously over his shoulder at the beam emitter that was making a gentle clicking sound as it cooled down.

'Woah,' he said as he peered into the hole. Clearly visible were a series of further holes beyond that got smaller and smaller with perspective. Dimly visible at the far end was what could only be a small circle of bright daylight.

'Erm, I don't know how to tell you this, Franz,' Otto said, turning towards his friend with a broad grin on his face, 'but it looks like you just made a hole in the school.'

'Oh dear,' Professor Pike said, coming up beside Otto and also peering into the hole. 'I do hope that we haven't damaged anything important.'

'Or any*one* important,' Shelby added as she and the rest of the Alphas gathered round.

'It is not being my fault,' Franz moaned. 'I am tripping over the cable.'

A couple of minutes later, the door at the far end of the lab hissed open and Chief Dekker came running into the room, flanked by two guards in their familiar orange jumpsuits. Otto and the others winced as they saw her. It was well known already that she had no particular love for H.I.V.E.'s Alpha stream and she seemed to have a special dislike for their year in particular.

'What happened?' she demanded as she strode across the room towards the Professor. Her thin, tight lips and sharp cheekbones gave the impression that she was someone who'd heard of this thing called smiling but had decided that it was not for her.

'There was a slight . . . erm . . . malfunction,' the Professor replied with a fleeting glance in Franz's direction. 'Has anyone been injured?'

'It doesn't look like it,' Dekker replied tersely, 'but I think it's safe to say that Colonel Francisco won't be using that particular toilet cubicle again.' Franz visibly paled at the thought of the Colonel finding out that he had been in any way responsible for whatever indignity he had just suffered. He had a sudden horribly clear vision of many laps of the school gym somewhere in his not too distant future.

'Please apologise to the Colonel for me,' the Professor said quickly, seeing the expression on Franz's face. 'I take full responsibility. I must not have secured the shielding properly.'

'You're sure there was no student involvement?' Dekker asked, glaring at Otto and the others.

'Quite sure,' the Professor replied. 'Now if there's nothing else I can help you with, we should start clearing this mess up.'

Dekker stared at Otto for a couple more seconds and then turned and marched out of the room.

'Oh, she's definitely got the hots for you,' Shelby whispered to Otto as the door hissed shut behind the new Security Chief.

'Yeah, great, just what I need,' Otto sighed.

'OK, everyone,' Professor Pike said, 'class is dismissed until we get this mess sorted out. Please use the rest of the morning for constructive study. Remember that you all have exams coming up.'

Otto and the others headed out of the lab, leaving Professor Pike to coordinate with the maintenance and repair team that had just arrived.

'Good work, Franz,' Shelby said with a grin. 'I've always said that H.I.V.E. needed more windows.'

'I am just being glad that Colonel Francisco will not discover that I was being involved,' Franz said, shaking his head.

'Yeah,' Otto said with a chuckle, 'but I would have paid good money to see the look on his face when it happened.'

'At least no one was hurt,' Laura said. 'That's the main thing.'

'Indeed,' Wing said with a nod, 'though I am not sure that it is a positive thing that what qualifies as a good day at H.I.V.E. is one where no one was either killed or permanently maimed.'

'So are you guys going to head to the library?' Nigel asked. 'Beause I could do with a hand with some of the political and financial corruption coursework. I still don't understand some of the corporate banking loopholes.'

'Does anyone?' Otto asked.

'I can be helping with those,' Franz said happily. 'It is actually being quite simple.'

'I'm glad you think so,' Shelby said with a sigh. 'It might as well be a foreign language to me.'

Franz had actually always shown a talent for that particular sphere of villainy. He excelled in developing new and inventive ways of hiding and then discreetly distributing vast sums of money. It was a subject that even Otto found baffling at times but it seemed to be almost second nature to Franz.

The six of them made their way through H.I.V.E.'s twisting volcanic rock corridors until they eventually arrived at the library. The large glass double doors, engraved with G.L.O.V.E.'s globe-smashing fist logo hissed apart and they headed inside. The cavernous chamber beyond was filled from floor to ceiling with countless shelves of books. Robotic arms slid backwards and forwards along rails mounted in front of the shelves, removing and returning volumes for the students who sat at the hundreds of desks arranged in clusters across the cavern floor. There was a definite atmosphere of barely suppressed panic that could only mean one thing. Exams were coming and time for revision was running out.

Otto and the others sat at the far end of the room and started unpacking notepads and books from their backpacks.

'Isn't all this studying a bit pointless if the plan to . . . borrow the exam papers works?' Laura whispered to Otto as he sat down and opened one of his textbooks.

'Maybe,' Otto whispered, 'but we have to keep up appearances.' He nodded towards one of the many security cameras that lined the walls. 'They're going to be looking out for anyone who's not bothering with revision. We need to try not to attract any unnecessary attention. Besides which, if the plan goes wrong, I don't want to be going into the exams having done absolutely no revision at all. I don't know about you but that's the kind of thing I have nightmares about.'

'I am having nightmares about sitting my exams naked,' Franz said with an earnest expression as he sat down across from them. 'Most disturbing.'

'If it's any consolation I have nightmares about Franz sitting exams naked too,' Shelby whispered to Laura. 'One's where I'm sat at the desk right behind his.'

'Oh, thanks very much for *that* mental image. Especially when I'm trying to concentrate,' Laura said.

'Thing is,' Shelby whispered, 'in the dream he's really nervous because of the exam and so he's sweating a *lot*.'

'OK, I am really not listening to you any more,' Laura said, grimacing.

'It gets worse because then he . . .' Shelby leant over and whispered something in Laura's ear.

'Is Laura OK?' Wing asked Otto quietly on the other side of the cluster of desks. 'She appears to have suddenly gone quite pale.'

Otto looked over at Laura who was now repeatedly hitting Shelby with one of her notepads. Shelby meanwhile was laughing uncontrollably at the look of pure disgust on Laura's face.

'Shelby Trinity, there is something seriously wrong with you,' Laura said, shaking her head.

'You know, I am thinking Laura is struggling to be coping with the stress of the exams,' Franz said sadly as he watched Laura rubbing at her temples as if desperately trying to erase something from her brain.

'It was an unfortunate accident,' Professor Pike said, looking slightly uncomfortable.

'That's one way of describing it,' Dr Nero said as he studied the damage report on his tablet display. He walked to the other end of the Science and Technology lab and examined the recently patched hole in the wall. 'I don't really want to have to review the safety procedures for your department yet again, Professor. Especially when you've been doing so well with the departmental fatalities.'

'Only three this year!' the Professor said, smiling happily before noticing the look on Nero's face. 'Which is, of course, three too many.'

'A certain level of staff and student mortality is to be expected, Professor,' Nero said, 'but it's best if we can try and avoid it where possible. Colonel Francisco was extremely lucky.'

'Yes, he seemed rather angry when I saw him,' the Professor said with a frown. 'He said that it was a good job he was sitting down when it happened. I suppose it must have been quite a shock for him.'

'Yes, I think that's safe to say,' Nero replied. The lab door hissed open and Chief Dekker marched into the room. 'Ahh, Chief, you said you wanted to see me.'

'Yes, Doctor Nero,' Dekker replied. 'I want to request that I be allowed to put some new security measures in place in the lead up to the examinations. I've been running inventory checks and some unusual pieces of equipment have gone missing from the school storerooms. I'd like your permission to search certain students' quarters and see what they might be hiding.'

'Absolutely not,' Nero said, shaking his head.

'But, sir,' Dekker said, 'if we don't . . .'

'Chief Dekker,' Nero said firmly, interrupting her, 'you have only been with the school for a few months so I am aware that there are still certain things that you may find difficult to understand, so allow me to explain. H.I.V.E. is not a prison. Certainly the students are brought here against their will and they are most definitely not allowed to leave except under the closest of supervision but that is where the similarities end. The students are entitled to a certain amount of freedom and privacy and that is why I have made it the policy of this institution that students' quarters are not to be searched unless there is unequivocal proof of a direct threat to the safety of the school. That may seem like a strange decision to you but it is my belief that if we treat our students like common criminals that is exactly how they will behave. What I want H.I.V.E. to produce is *uncommon* criminals. No searches without my explicit permission and that is my final word on the matter. Do I make myself clear?'

'Yes, sir,' Dekker said with a curt nod. 'Understood. I do have one other concern though. I have reviewed the file on

Otto Malpense and if everything that I read about his abilities is true I'm worried that there is no meaningful way to secure the school's network against his intrusion. Given the sensitivity of the data that's stored there, how do we ensure that he won't be able to gain access to it?'

'H.I.V.E.mind,' the Professor replied. 'You will have read, no doubt, about everything that took place during our final confrontation with Overlord. So you will know that H.I.V.E.mind was stored temporarily within the organic computer that is implanted inside Otto's brain. One of the side effects of that has been that H.I.V.E.mind is now uniquely attuned to Malpense's brain patterns. As long as H.I.V.E.mind is active there is no way that Otto can access the school's networks using his abilities without being immediately detected. One of H.I.V.E.mind's prime directives is to protect certain pieces of sensitive data at all costs. The examination papers are one such piece of data. Otto can't access them with his abilities and he will know that.'

'Nevertheless, my instincts tell me that he's up to something,' Dekker said with a frown. 'I'm not sure what yet but if I could just search his quarters . . .'

'You're almost certainly correct, Chief,' Nero said with a slight smile, 'but, to be honest, I'd be more worried if your instincts were telling you that he wasn't up to something. Otto Malpense's default state is "up to something" and I would have it no other way. Is there anything else?'

'No, sir,' Dekker replied.

'Very well. If you do find positive evidence of whatever it is that Mr Malpense is planning, then do please let me know. I'm sure it will be entertaining at the very least.'

Dekker nodded and marched out of the room.

'I don't much like her, Max,' the Professor said as the lab door hissed shut behind the Chief.

'I didn't think many people would. Chief Lewis was a difficult man to replace,' Nero said. 'However, she comes highly recommended and she's exceptionally good at what she does and just at the moment I need someone who will keep this school safe. No matter what the cost.'

☢ ☢ ☢

Raven watched from the monitoring station in the belly of the Shroud as retrieval teams all around the world provided constant status updates on their operations. She was not the sort of person to suffer from stress but this was the one occasion every year which, she conceded, she found slightly worrying. Part of it was that there was no way that she could be there for each retrieval operation personally but the other part was that she knew how important it was to Nero that every one of these children be retrieved successfully. She had stopped worrying about the rights and wrongs of recruiting H.I.V.E.'s new students in this way many years ago. They were being saved from lives of mediocrity and being given the sort of opportunity that would change their lives for the better for ever. Besides which, all of them had done something to earn their place at H.I.V.E. None of them were angels.

She continued to scan the reports coming in. She wasn't worried about the legacy student retrievals. They were simple since they occurred with the full knowledge of the parents or guardians of the children involved. No, the tricky ones were the other students, the children who had earned their place through merit, if that was really the right word under the circumstances. Those were the operations that Raven watched most closely.

'Team nine, retrieval complete,' a voice crackled over the comms system. Team nine, Brazilian girl, ran a team of pickpockets in the favela. Exceptional leadership skills, master of stealth and evasion, highly adept thief. Alpha stream candidate.

'Team seventeen, retrieval complete,' another voice reported. Team seventeen, American boy, son of a wealthy banker. Siphoned nearly a million dollars from the accounts of his father and his golf club buddies by cloning their credit cards while they were out on the fairways. Politics and Finance stream candidate.

'Team twenty-nine, retrieval complete.' Russian boy, assassin for the mob. Used age as cover to get close to targets. Highly skilled with pistols and knives. Henchman stream candidate. That was one she'd been worried about.

And so the reports continued to roll in. No problems so far but there was plenty of time yet.

'We're over the target area,' a voice in her earpiece said.

'Roger that,' Raven replied, pulling the black mask over her head. The black lenses activated, giving her perfect twenty-twenty, full-colour night vision. She walked towards the rear of the passenger compartment and checked her equipment rig one last time. Satisfied that everything was in place she slapped the hatch release and stepped out on to the ramp. The ground was only a couple of metres below and she jumped down and landed silently.

'Raven down,' she reported. 'Clear and stay on station.'

'Roger,' the pilot of the Shroud replied as the hatch whirred shut and the Shroud climbed silently to a holding altitude.

Raven checked her surroundings. The surveillance team had reported that her targets had entered the underground parking garage just a few minutes earlier. Targets, plural – that was why she was here. Double retrievals were unusual and difficult. She ran down the ramp and scanned the garage, her lenses instantly adjusting to compensate for the fluorescent strip lighting overhead. She heard the roar of a powerful engine from one of the lower floors and flattened herself against one of the support columns next to the exit

57

ramp. She peered round the column's edge just in time to see an expensive Italian sports car power-sliding round the corner at the far end of the garage. Raven took a deep breath and stepped out into the middle of the exit ramp.

The driver of the car instinctively swerved to avoid the black-clad figure that suddenly stepped out into the road in front of him. As the car shot past her Raven's swords flashed and the front right wheel disintegrated. The car went out of control and drove straight into another vehicle parked beside the ramp with a crunch. Both the air bags in the car deployed with a bang and Raven ran for the driver's door, pulling the Sleeper pistol from the holster on her thigh. The driver was halfway out of the car when there was a zapping sound and the Sleeper's neural shock pulse dropped him unconscious to the floor.

Raven moved quickly round the car and saw that the passenger door was already open. Suddenly a girl with bright pink hair popped up from behind the car that the sports car had driven into. There was something in her hand. Raven twisted instinctively as there was a popping sound and two darts, trailing wires, shot from the object the girl was holding. The darts struck Raven in the shoulder, triggering the taser's massive electrical discharge, sending Raven to her knees. She cursed under her breath in Russian as she fought to stay conscious, reaching slowly for the two wires that trailed from the darts embedded in her skin.

Fighting to control her convulsing muscles she took a firm hold of the wires, gritted her teeth and pulled. The young girl watched in wide-eyed astonishment as Raven threw the darts to the ground and slowly got to her feet.

'That hurt,' Raven said, raising the Sleeper.

chapter four

Otto sat down next to Laura, placing his tray on the table. She was reading a book filled with circuit diagrams and technical schematics.

'Any good jokes in that?' Otto asked with a smile.

'Oh yeah,' Laura replied. 'Intercontinental ballistic missile guidance systems are a real laugh fest.'

'I can imagine,' Otto said, sticking a fork into the food on his plate. The dining room was bustling with lunchtime activity. All around them students from each of H.I.V.E.'s streams were eating and chatting. It was one of the few times that the streams mixed like this but even now most of the tables arranged around the giant cavern were occupied by groups from just one stream. Nearby a group of Henchman students in their distinctive blue jumpsuits were sitting round a table having a noisy argument about exactly who had achieved the most kills in their latest holographic combat training session. Next to them was a table filled with students from the Science and Technology stream who were having a much quieter discussion about the differing properties of various forms of thermal shielding for reactor cores. They all wore white jumpsuits and would occasionally glance nervously at the Henchman students at the next table. Otto didn't blame them for feeling slightly uncomfortable. The members of the Henchman stream were notorious for their constant bullying of students from the other groups. They had an unpleasant habit of picking on the SciTech students in particular or as they called them, 'the nerd stream'. Otto sometimes wondered why Dr Nero tolerated the aggressive behaviour of the Henchman students. He supposed there had to be a reason – with Nero there seemed to always be a reason for everything.

'I've been thinking about our plan,' Otto said quietly. 'I think we should do it sooner rather than later. I'm getting nervous about the special attention we're getting from Dekker.'

'Aye,' Laura replied, 'I know what you mean. If we're going to do this we'd better do it before she puts us all under lockdown.'

'I'm thinking tomorrow night,' Otto said. 'Do you think you'll have finished the new code for the device by then?'

'There's just a couple of bugs to be worked out,' Laura replied, glancing around to make sure that they were not being eavesdropped on. 'We can't risk hooking it up until we're one hundred per cent sure that Big Blue won't feel it.'

Big Blue was Laura's affectionate nickname for H.I.V.E.mind. He was much more than just a piece of software, acting as he did as a digital guardian, protecting and securing the entire school. He had also become a friend to Otto and the others, saving all of their lives on more than one occasion.

'Yeah, well, we wouldn't have to be bothering with all of this if he'd just been a little bit more cooperative,' Otto said.

'Oh, come on, Otto, you didn't really expect him to just give you the exam papers because you asked him nicely, did you?'

'It was worth a try. He still owes me,' Otto replied.

'You know he can't ignore a direct command from Nero,' Laura said. 'It's not his fault.'

'I know,' Otto said with a sigh. 'Now we're just going to have to do it the hard way.'

'I think it's been more fun this way actually,' Laura replied with a smile. 'I've really enjoyed us working on the device together. I mean . . . the intellectual challenge of it . . . you know.'

'Yeah, me too,' Otto said. 'It's been fun doing it the old-fashioned way.'

'What do you mean *old fashioned*?' Laura said with mock indignation. 'I'll have you know that this is cutting-edge stuff we've been working on.'

'Cutting edge for *you* maybe . . .' Otto said with a grin.

'Right, that's it, no more soldering for you, my boy,' Laura said, folding her arms and leaning back in her chair. 'I'm revoking your tinkering privileges.'

'I'm not interrupting anything, am I?' a voice with an American accent asked from behind Otto.

Otto turned round and saw a tall boy with neatly trimmed brown hair standing behind him. His grey jumpsuit marked him out as a student from the Politics and Finance stream and the pips in his collar indicated that he was in his fifth year at the H.I.V.E. Otto had seen him around on occasion but he had no idea who he was.

'Hi,' the boy said with a smile, extending his hand. 'I don't think we've met. I'm Cole Harrington and you must be the infamous Otto Malpense. Mind if I join you?'

'Actually we were just having a conversation,' Otto said, glancing back at Laura.

'It's fine,' Laura said, putting her book in her backpack and picking up her lunch tray. 'I need to go and do some revision anyway. I'll catch up with you later, Otto.' She glanced over at Harrington who was sitting down in the seat opposite Otto and raised a quizzical eyebrow as she left.

'It's a pleasure to finally meet you in person,' Harrington said, still smiling. 'I've heard a lot of stories about you.'

'Most of them not true, I'm sure,' Otto replied. There were comparatively few people at H.I.V.E. who really knew the precise details of the incidents that Otto had been involved in since his arrival at H.I.V.E. and so the rumour mill had filled in the blanks with little regard for accuracy. If Otto had actually done half of the things that he was supposed to have done then he would have either been expelled or executed long before now. Although, in fairness, at H.I.V.E. they were often essentially the same thing.

'Maybe, but my sources tell me that you're still a very useful person to know,' Cole said, 'especially with the exams coming up, if you know what I mean.'

'I've got no idea what you're talking about,' Otto said, suddenly feeling slightly uncomfortable.

'Of course you don't. Humour me for a moment though and just pretend that you do. Let's just imagine that actually you have some sort of plan for getting hold of the exam questions. And then, having imagined that, let's also imagine that there was someone who might be able to reward you handsomely for sharing that information with him. Can you imagine that, Otto?'

'Oh, I have a very active imagination,' Otto replied, 'but what makes you think that I would be interested in sharing any such information with my new imaginary friend? It's

64

not like there's anything he could offer that I really need. Not while I'm stuck here at least.'

'That's just where you're wrong,' Harrington said. 'There are all sorts of ways that a person's life at H.I.V.E. can be made easier.' He paused for a moment, the previous friendly warmth in his expression suddenly vanishing, replaced by something much colder and harder. 'Just as there are all sorts of ways that a person's life at H.I.V.E. can be made much, much harder.'

'Are you threatening me?' Otto asked, looking Harrington straight in the eye.

'Of course not,' Harrington replied, the broad smile returning. 'I'm just clarifying your options for you.'

'Good,' Otto replied, 'because it would have been really, *really* stupid of you to threaten me.'

'Is everything OK here?' Wing asked as he approached the table and noticed the expression on Otto's face.

'Everything's fine,' Harrington said as he stood up. 'We were just discussing a little business. Do let me know what you decide, Otto. I'm sure you'll make the right decision.'

'Who was that?' Wing asked as he watched Harrington walk away.

'A future President of the United States,' Otto replied with a frown, 'and just possibly a really big problem.'

Raven tightened the final strap on the stretcher, making sure that the unconscious boy lying on it was firmly secured. She checked the pulse on his neck and was pleased to feel that it was steady and strong. The Sleeper guns were designed to incapacitate their targets as safely as possible but she did not want to take any chances. She moved further along the Shroud's passenger compartment and repeated the check on the young girl who had tasered her. She had a small bruise on her cheekbone from falling against the car when Raven had hit her with the Sleeper but nothing more serious than that. Raven had to admit to a grudging respect for the speed and accuracy of the girl's shot with the taser. It wasn't often that someone caught her by surprise like that.

Raven headed back to her seat and picked up the tablet displaying the latest reports from the retrieval teams. Everything seemed to be progressing smoothly. The vast majority of the operations had been completed successfully and there had only been a couple of minor injuries. Nero would be pleased. She placed the tablet back on the seat and climbed up the ladder to the Shroud's flight deck. The two pilots sat in the darkened cockpit, the only illumination provided by the banks of video displays and hundreds of illuminated switches that lined the control panel in front of them.

'How long until we're back at H.I.V.E.?' Raven asked.

'Three hours,' the pilot replied.

'Good,' Raven said. 'Notify me when we're five minutes out.'

'Understood,' the pilot replied with a nod.

Raven climbed back down to the lower deck and sat on one of the seats opposite the young girl. She looked like she was simply in a deep sleep, her chest rising and falling rhythmically, her expression peaceful. Raven watched her for a few minutes before she closed her eyes and leant back in her seat. She was too wired to sleep but she had taught herself over the years to use these moments of rest to clear her mind and centre herself. Normally it was easy but for some reason tonight she was finding it difficult. She could not shake off the image of the girl's face from earlier that evening as she had pulled the trigger on the taser. Unafraid, determined, efficient. It reminded her of something, a place that she had tried very hard to forget over the years. Tonight though, for whatever reason, she could not stop the memories flooding back. Memories of the past. Memories of the Glasshouse . . .

eighteen years ago

'Natalya,' the boy whispered, urgently shaking the shoulder of the girl lying on the top of the steel-framed bunk. 'Natalya, wake up!'

'What is it, Tolya?' Natalya groaned as she reluctantly opened her eyes. The boy standing next to her bed was looking round anxiously. They would both be punished if they were caught talking after lights out and she was already physically exhausted by the day's training without adding punishment exercises on top of everything else.

'It's Dimitri, he's gone,' Tolya whispered.

'What do you mean "gone"?' Natalya asked, pushing herself up in her bed and looking down the dormitory that was only dimly lit by the watery moonlight pouring through the skylights far overhead.

'I mean he's gone, not here, vanished, what do you think I mean?' Tolya said impatiently. 'A noise woke me up and when I looked across at Dimitri's bunk it was empty.'

'If this is some kind of joke, Tolya, I'm telling you now that it's not very funny,' Natalya whispered, getting up out of her bunk. The pair of them crept through the room as quietly as they could. It was always cold in the dormitory and the plain cotton pyjamas that they wore did little to keep them warm now that they were out from under the heavy woollen blankets on their beds. They arrived at Dimitri's bunk and sure enough, it was quite empty.

'You checked the toilet?' Natalya asked, nodding towards the door in the corner of the room.

'No, I suppose he could be in there,' Tolya replied.

'Tolya, you idiot,' Natalya said with a sigh, 'if you've woken me up just because Dimitri needed a pee I am going to hurt you really quite badly.'

Natalya walked over to the door to the bathroom and looked inside.

'Dimitri,' she whispered, 'are you in here?' There was no reply. She walked down the long line of cubicle doors and checked that none were occupied.

'See, he's not here,' Tolya said, sounding rather relieved.

'Then where is he?' Natalya said. 'He can't have just vanished into thin air.'

Suddenly something caught her eye.

'What's that?' she asked, pointing into the gloom.

'What?' Tolya said, looking in the direction she indicated but seeing nothing.

Natalya walked over to the corner of the room and with a rush of excitement she realised what it was. Hanging down from one of the bracing girders that ran across the space below the skylights was a thin rope. Natalya tugged on the rope experimentally and found that it felt firmly attached.

'Where'd that come from?' Tolya asked.

'The rope fairy must have left it,' Natalya said.

'What?'

'It's Dimitri, you idiot,' Natalya said impatiently. 'He must have found a way out.'

'Up there?' Tolya said with a look of disbelief.

'Only one way to find out,' Natalya said as she grabbed the rope and began to haul herself towards the ceiling. She stopped halfway up and looked down at Tolya who was standing at the bottom of the rope looking extremely nervous. 'Come on,' she said, 'what are you afraid of?'

'It's not what I'm afraid of,' Tolya muttered to himself as he grabbed the bottom of the rope, 'it's who.'

Natalya reached the top of the rope and hauled herself up on to the dusty girder. It was probably only ten metres to the concrete below but that seemed quite a long way down from up here. She could also see the rows of bunks on the other side of the partition wall that separated them from the toilets and she was glad to see that no one else seemed to have been woken by their creeping around. A few moments later Tolya pulled himself up on to the girder beside her.

'Where did Dimitri manage to find a grapple?' Tolya asked quietly as Natalya examined the hook that secured the rope to the girder. Natalya had no idea but then she rarely had any idea how Dimitri managed to get his hands on the things that he did. He had been one of the first friends she had made when she arrived at the Glasshouse two years ago and without him and Tolya, Natalya doubted that she would have survived the first six months. He was one of the few people she knew who had not had his spirit broken by this place and she loved him for it.

'We can ask him when we find him, can't we?' Natalya said with a smile. 'Look.' She pointed over at one of the nearby skylights. The padlock that had secured it hung open and it was propped open, just a crack, with a thin piece of wood. Natalya crept carefully along the girder towards the skylight. She slid her fingers into the narrow gap and lifted it open very slowly as its old hinges creaked in protest.

'Come on,' Natalya said, as she stepped on to the roof outside, holding the skylight open for Tolya. He hesitated for a moment, looking uncertain. 'This could be our chance to get out of here.'

'OK,' Tolya said with a slight shake of the head as he climbed out after her, 'but I must be crazy.'

'After two years in this place I think crazy is actually pretty normal,' Natalya replied as she crouched down and crept over to the parapet that ran along the edge of the roof. She peered over the top of the dirty brickwork and down into the moonlit courtyard below. Everything seemed quiet. There were no signs of any unusual activity. Beyond the courtyard was the perimeter wall and she watched as the guards who were supposed to be patrolling it, stood sharing a cigarette and chatting. On the other side of the wall was another fence and beyond that many miles of frozen forest. They wouldn't make it more than a couple of miles in the pyjamas they were wearing, so their first priority had to be finding warmer clothes. She knew that there was a storeroom on the east side of the courtyard that held just what they needed. Now all she had to do was figure out how to get down there.

'What now?' Tolya asked as he too peered down into the snow-covered courtyard.

'First we need to . . .' Natalya stopped as the courtyard was suddenly flooded with bright, white light. A small figure bolted out of the storeroom she had just been planning to loot and sprinted across the cobbles towards the perimeter wall. He was wearing full survival kit with one pack on his back and was carrying another two bulging packs, one in each hand.

'Dimitri!' Natalya gasped as she recognised the boy running across the brightly lit square. There were shouts from the guards on the wall as they raised their rifles to their shoulders. Dimitri slowed to a halt, dropping the other two packs to the ground and raising his hands in surrender.

'What's he doing?' Tolya asked, sounding bewildered.

'You idiot, Dimitri,' Natalya said under her breath. 'Why do you always have to play the hero? We should have all gone together.' But she knew what he had done. He had been trying to get the gear that all three of them would need to escape. He had more chance of successfully escaping on his own but he was going to come back and take her and Tolya with him. That was why he had propped the skylight open and left the rope in place instead of taking it with him.

'Oh no,' Tolya whispered as he recognised the two figures that were walking out of the front door of the compound's main building. Anastasia and Pietor Furan. They walked towards Dimitri who stood his ground defiantly, head held high. Pietor Furan raised his hand and delivered a scything backhand fist to the boy's jaw, knocking him to one knee. Dimitri slowly stood back up as Anastasia put a restraining hand on her brother's arm. She began to talk to Dimitri and Natalya strained to make out any details of the conversation from her high vantage point but it was pointless, they were too far away. Her mind raced as she watched the scene unfolding below. There had to be something she could do to help him. Anastasia turned away from Dimitri and reached inside her long white coat. Natalya felt the scream issuing unbidden from her lips as she saw the woman raising a pistol towards Dimitri's chest.

'Nooooo!' Natalya screamed, standing up and watching powerlessly as Anastasia Furan's head turned slowly towards her. The woman stared at Natalya, looking her straight in the eye as she pulled the trigger. Natalya felt her legs give way underneath her as Dimitri fell backwards, the white snow blooming with crimson red beneath him.

Natalya sank to the floor, turning her back against the parapet and wrapping her arms round her knees. She sat there staring vacantly into space as Tolya, tears streaming down his face, grabbed her by the shoulders and shook her.

'Natalya, please, we have to run, now!' he pleaded, knowing in his heart that there was really nowhere to run to. She didn't offer any resistance as the guards poured out of the nearby door on to the roof and dragged her down the stairs to the courtyard. What was the point? The guards hauled her across the snow-covered cobbles and threw her to the ground in front of Anastasia Furan. The older woman leant down and cupped Natalya's chin in her hand, raising her face until she was looking directly into her eyes.

'What a terrible waste,' Anastasia said as she looked towards Dimitri's body, 'of a bullet.'

Deep inside Natalya something broke, something that would never again be truly whole. She let out a scream that turned the nearby guards' faces pale as she launched herself at Anastasia Furan with every intention of killing her where she stood with nothing but her bare hands. Pietor slammed Natalya to the ground, pinning her against the cold cobbles as she fought fruitlessly to get free. Tolya could do nothing but watch in horror as he saw his friend Natalya replaced by someone . . . no, something . . . different.

'I wondered how long it would take us to find the animal inside you, Natalya,' Anastasia said, a chilling smile on her face. 'And now I have my answer.' More guards helped Pietor to restrain the feral girl. 'Take them both to the detention block,' Anastasia said with a dismissive wave as she turned to leave. 'Indefinite isolation.'

☻☻☻

There was no such thing as time to Natalya any more. There was no daytime or night-time, just unrelenting blackness that was broken for a few seconds each day by the shaft of light that poured into the cell through the hole in the door when the guards used to give her food and water. She slept only fitfully – the nightmares that plagued her were too terrible to grant her even that refuge.

Days passed, then weeks, or so she guessed. There was no way of knowing for sure. There was a part of her that just wanted to fade away, here in the darkness, shrinking to nothingness, but there was another, stronger voice in her head. That voice told her to hold on, to not let the despair and the isolation break her. She had a mission, one that only she could complete and so she could not surrender to the pain. Killing Anastasia Furan, that was all that mattered. She would not let them break her, she would not give them the satisfaction.

Then, one day, without warning, the door to her cell was opened. There was no one on the other side, just a corridor that seemed impossibly bright. She stepped out into the light, squinting in pain as the glaring brightness seemed to almost press down on her. The door at the far end of the

75

corridor was open and she walked slowly towards it. Beyond that door was a circular room, its smooth concrete walls leading up to a caged gallery ten metres above. As Natalya entered the room the door slammed shut behind her and locked. She stood staring up at the gallery above as Anastasia and Pietor Furan appeared.

Natalya tried to speak, but her voice was little more than a croaky whisper. It had been a long time since she had used it.

'What was that, Natalya?' Anastasia said with a smile.

'I said you should have killed me,' Natalya whispered.

'No, Natalya,' Anastasia replied, 'you have too much potential for that. I saw it in you the first time we met. Call it instinct if you like but I can always spot a killer. I look at you and I see myself many years ago.'

'I am nothing like you,' Natalya said, her voice seeming to grow stronger again each time she used it.

'Not yet perhaps, but you will be in time and today you take the first proper step on that path.'

The door set in the opposite room of the circular pit swung open and a barely recognisable figure staggered into the room.

'Tolya,' Natalya gasped. There was no hint of recognition in his eyes as he looked at her, just a terrible blank stare that made the hairs stand up on the back of her neck. 'What have they done to you?'

'He has received exactly the same punishment as you, my dear,' Anastasia said, 'but I'm afraid he lacks your strength. They say that if you leave a person in darkness for long enough they will always carry some of that darkness around inside them. I fear that in this poor boy's case it has consumed him.'

Tolya made a terrible low guttural growling noise, more beast than human and he ran at Natalya. She dodged to one side, pushing him away from her and into the wall. He spun and lunged back towards her with an infuriated roar and she backed away, circling him, trying to stay out of his reach.

'Tolya, it's me, Natalya,' she said as they circled each other. 'We're friends, please, try to remember.'

'Let's speed things up shall we,' Anastasia said as she watched Natalya duck away from another of Tolya's lunging grabs. She signalled to Furan and he opened a section of the cage that surrounded the upper walkway and threw two objects into the centre of the pit. Natalya stared at the gleaming pair of blades that lay on the floor between her and Tolya. He dashed forward and snatched the twin katanas from the floor before Natalya could react. She ducked backwards as he swung the blades wildly at her. She felt the concrete wall at her back and he lunged. The tip of one of the blades sliced into her cheek, leaving a long curved gash, and she hit back blindly, punching him in the face. Tolya staggered backwards as Natalya advanced feeling the blood trickling down her cheek. The training she had received over the last two long years suddenly kicked in and she delivered a series of precise punches and kicks to Tolya's torso. He flailed at her with one of the swords and she ducked beneath the wild swing and jabbed at his wrist, paralysing his hand and sending the blade clattering away across the floor. He swung at her again with the other katana and she ducked beneath the sweeping blade and rolled towards the sword lying on the floor. She scooped it up, despite the fact she had never fought with a sword in her life, and turned back towards Tolya who charged at her with an animal roar. She brought her sword up in a vain effort to defend herself as he hit her like a freight train and she felt a sudden, shuddering impact run through her weapon. She struggled to throw him off her as she felt his hands closing around her throat and squeezing. She couldn't breathe, feeling panic as the fringes of her vision started to blacken. Then Tolya's grip slackened and just for a moment Natalya thought she saw a flicker of recognition in her friend's eyes. He gave a small pained gasp and then collapsed on top of Natalya with a final rasping sigh. Natalya rolled Tolya's limp body off from on top of her and staggered to her feet. She grabbed the hilt of the katana that protruded from her dead friend's chest and pulled it free before picking Tolya's sword up from the floor.

She looked up at Anastasia Furan, half her face covered in blood and with a sword in each hand. She didn't say anything, she didn't need to, her expression made the depth of her hatred perfectly clear.

'She's going to be dangerous,' Pietor Furan said, looking down at Natalya.

'No, Pietor, she is going to be magnificent,' Anastasia replied with a smile.

☻☻☻

now

Raven caught the Shroud's co-pilot's wrist in a vice-like grip a moment before he actually touched her shoulder. For a fleeting instant there was a look of such unbridled malevolence in her eyes that he felt his heart quicken but then her expression softened.

'I'm sorry to wake you,' the man said slightly nervously.

'I wasn't asleep,' Raven replied, trying to shake off the feeling of lingering despair that always accompanied the memories of her childhood. 'Are we nearly home?'

'Yes, ma'am,' the co-pilot replied with a nod. 'Five minutes.'

'Thank you,' Raven replied, standing up and heading over to the stretchers on the opposite side of the passenger compartment. She checked the unconscious boy's pulse – still strong.

'I know you're awake,' Raven said to the girl in the other stretcher, smiling to herself. 'So feigning unconsciousness will not catch me off guard.' The girl's head turned so that she could see Raven.

'Where are you taking me?' the girl asked, straining against the straps that secured her to the stretcher.

'You'll find out very soon,' Raven replied. 'If you stop struggling, I'll undo those straps.'

The girl stared at Raven for a moment and then lay still. Raven moved over to her stretcher and released the straps one by one. The girl sat up and looked at Raven, as if sizing her up.

'Who are you?' the girl asked, frowning slightly.

'You may call me Raven.'

'Why have you kidnapped us? Who do you work for?' the girl demanded. Raven could not help but admire her apparent lack of fear.

'Let's just say that I work in . . . recruitment,' Raven replied with a slight smile.

'Recruitment for what?' the girl asked, looking round the dimly lit interior of the Shroud.

The boy in the other stretcher let out a low moan and his eyes fluttered open. Raven moved over to his stretcher, undid the restraining straps and helped him to sit up. He was tall and handsome with a thick mop of brown hair that hung down over his forehead and his dark brown eyes. He seemed totally disorientated for a moment or two and then his eyes widened and he pushed himself back against the bulkhead away from Raven.

'What's going on?' he said, sounding bewildered.

'I've already asked her that,' the girl said as she sat down next to the confused-looking boy. 'I'm afraid straight answers don't seem to be her speciality.'

There was a sudden soft thud as the Shroud touched down and Raven moved over to the boarding ramp release switch.

'You're about to get all the answers you could possibly want,' Raven said as she hit the button and the ramp began to descend. 'Please, after you,' she said, gesturing for them to proceed.

The girl helped the boy get unsteadily to his feet and they walked down the slope. At the bottom were several security guards armed with Sleepers.

'This way please,' one of the guards said, gesturing for them to follow. They followed him without question, eyes wide and mouths hanging open in amazement as they tried to take in the scene that greeted them. Dozens of sleek, black insectile dropships like the one they had just disembarked from were spread out around the floor of the huge hangar that surrounded them. There was a rumble from high overhead and they looked up to see two massive reinforced shutters sliding together far above them, sealing them inside the enormous floodlit cavern. Several other children were climbing down from the strange aircraft and following security guards across the hangar floor towards a massive opening in the rocky wall. They shared the same look of dumbstruck awe.

'All retrieval teams report for debriefing,' a soft, vaguely synthetic voice said over speakers hidden somewhere in the walls. 'All flight crews to perform post-flight checks.'

Raven watched as the pair of new students who she had recruited joined the group of twenty or so other children who were being herded towards the main meeting hall by their security team escorts. She followed along behind, quietly taking up a position at the back of the enormous cavern that was used for all full school assemblies. There was a low-level buzz of nervous chatter now as the new intake of students was arranged in lines in front of the lectern at the far end of the room. Behind the lectern was a sculpture depicting a fist hammering down upon a cracked globe, the symbol of G.L.O.V.E. At its base was inscribed the G.L.O.V.E. motto: 'Do Unto Others'.

A moment later the door at the side of the stage hissed open and Dr Nero strode over to the lectern. He paused for a moment, looking at the array of bewildered but curious faces that stared back at him.

'Good morning, ladies and gentlemen,' Nero began. 'Welcome to H.I.V.E. and the first day of the rest of your lives.'

chapter five

A few hours later the two new students who had been retrieved by Raven sat down on one of the sofas in the atrium of accommodation block seven looking exhausted and overwhelmed. They were both now wearing black Alpha stream jumpsuits.

'Well,' the boy said with a sigh, 'I think it's safe to say that today couldn't possibly get any weirder.'

'And that's just where you'd be wrong,' the girl said, looking at something over his shoulder, a broad grin spreading across her face. 'I don't believe it.' The boy stood up and turned round as his companion ran past him.

'What on earth are you doing here?' Otto said with a grin as the girl hugged him. The girl stepped back and the boy grabbed Otto by both shoulders.

'Jeez, Otto, we wondered where you'd got to, but I think

it's safe to say that this is just a bit stranger than any of the theories we came up with.'

'Are you gonna introduce us?' Shelby asked as she and Laura exchanged confused looks.

'Of course, sorry,' Otto replied. 'Guys, this is Tom and this is Penny and let's just say that we used to *work* together.'

'You mean we used to nick stuff for you,' Penny said with a grin.

'I was trying to make it sound more classy,' Otto replied with a chuckle.

'You guys knew each other before this place?' Laura asked, still looking slightly confused.

'Yeah and I suppose this is exactly the sort of place that I should have expected Otto to end up in when I actually stop and think about it. Penny Richards, pleased to meet you.' She stuck out her hand.

'Laura Brand,' Laura said, shaking her hand, 'and this is Shelby Trinity.'

'Hi,' Shelby said with a little wave.

'Hi to you too,' Tom said with a smile. 'Tom Ransom, a pleasure to meet you both.'

'So when did you get here?' Otto asked as they all sat down on the cluster of sofas.

'This morning,' Penny replied. 'Let's just say that it's been a pretty strange twenty-four hours.'

'I can imagine,' Otto said. 'I can see you had a bit of a rough day.' He gestured towards the bruise on Penny's cheekbone.

'Yeah, I think that Raven woman must not have been too pleased when I tasered her,' Penny replied with a lopsided grin.

'You are tasering Raven!' Franz said slightly too loudly as he sat down on the sofa. 'This is not being a clever thing to do.'

'That's one way of putting it,' Nigel said as he sat down next to Franz. 'Glad to see that you still have all your limbs at least.'

'I doubt that Raven would have resorted to dismember-ment except under circumstances of extreme provocation,' Wing said with a slight frown.

'I was jok— Never mind,' Nigel said, rolling his eyes.

'And here's the rest of our motley crew,' Otto said. 'Tom, Penny, this is Wing, Franz and Nigel.'

'A pleasure to meet you,' Wing said with a slight bow. 'I believe that Otto has mentioned you to me before. You lived in the same orphanage before he came to H.I.V.E. did you not?'

'Yeah,' Tom replied, 'good old St Sebastian's.'

'How is Mrs McReedy these days?' Otto asked.

'Fine, though she was rather sad to lose her best revenue stream when you disappeared,' Penny said.

Mrs McReedy had been the head of Otto's old orphanage or at least that was what she and Otto let the rest of the world believe. In reality Otto had been essentially running the place at the time he was recruited by H.I.V.E. while making sure that Mrs McReedy was living the affluently comfortable lifestyle to which she had become accustomed. They had an unspoken agreement that she should not enquire too closely about where the money for all her little luxuries had come from.

'So are you guys still living there?' Otto asked.

'No, we decided to make our own way in the world, if you know what I mean,' Tom replied. 'We'd had enough of the amount of money that some of the people in the City were getting paid so we started our own wealth redistribution programme.'

'The papers even gave us our own nickname "The Hoods",' Penny said with a grin, 'as in Robin Hood.'

'I have heard of this legend. He was a man with an admirable goal,' Wing said, 'stealing from the rich to give to the poor.'

'Yeah, we were just like him,' Tom said, suddenly looking slightly uncomfortable, 'except for the giving to the poor bit.'

'We were quite poor when we started,' Penny said defensively. 'And we did give some of it to charity . . . eventually.'

'And I suppose that's how you ended up getting our esteemed head teacher's attention,' Otto said, trying not to laugh at Wing's look of slightly confused disapproval.

'I suppose so,' Tom said, 'but, come on, Otto, tell us what exactly happened to you? You announce one day that you're going on a trip to the seaside and nobody hears anything from you ever again. I thought you'd finally got caught and ended up in some young offenders' institution somewhere.'

'Who says he didn't?' Laura said, gesturing at the surrounding walls.

'Let's just say that I got involved in politics,' Otto said with a grin. He decided that he didn't really want to go into too much detail about his part in the very public and very humiliating downfall of the British Prime Minister at that precise moment. Besides which, he'd probably caught Nero's attention well before the events of that particular day. That was just when Raven, quite literally, turned up on his doorstep.

'So what about the rest of you?' Penny asked. 'How did you all end up here?'

One by one they gave accounts of the various family connections or acts of nascent villainy that had led to them being recruited by H.I.V.E. Shelby was the last to explain her reasons for being at the school.

'I guess I was a bit like you guys,' she said with a smile. 'I was into what did you call it . . . wealth distribution too. I made a bit of a name for myself on the high value heist circuit. Before I came here people used to call me the Wraith.'

'OMG,' Penny gasped. 'You were the Wraith? Love your work! You have to tell me ... the Guggenheim job in Bilbao, how did you pull that off?'

'When we've got a spare couple of hours I'll give you all the details,' Shelby said smiling. 'Let's just say that it took me a week to get the smell of sewage out of my hair.'

'Ewww,' Laura said, wrinkling her nose.

'You don't know the half of it,' Shelby said, pulling a face. 'I thought there wouldn't be enough shampoo in the world.'

They were all still chatting as Carla Trieste, one of the senior year Alpha students, walked up to the group and interrupted.

'Glad to see that our new Alphas are making friends,' she said, 'but I'm supposed to show you two to your new sleeping quarters. Would you come with me please?'

'Suppose we'd better go and see who our new room-mates are going to be,' Penny said with a smile. 'Great to see you again, Otto, and it's been lovely to meet all of you guys. You know, this place suddenly doesn't seem quite so bad. Catch you later.'

'Yeah,' Tom said with a broad smile. 'Thanks for the warm welcome. See you all soon I hope.'

'Yum,' Shelby said as she watched Tom leave.

'Aye, he is quite easy on the eye,' Laura grinned, blushing slightly.

'Hmmm,' Wing said, frowning slightly.

'Awww, don't get jealous, big guy,' Shelby said putting her arm around him. 'You know I only have eyes for you. He's all yours, Brand.'

'I didn't mean that I wanted to . . . you know . . . well . . .' Laura said uncomfortably, her face going still redder.

'Yeah,' Otto said, 'why don't we let people settle in for a few days before we start arranging their love lives for them. Come on, Laura, let's go and finish the debugging on our project.'

'Awww, young nerds in love,' Shelby said, as Laura and Otto wandered off. 'You know, it's actually kinda cute.'

'I think it would perhaps be best if you were to refrain from teasing Laura like that,' Wing said. 'Not everyone wants you to select a romantic partner for them, you know.'

'Actually, I wouldn't be minding,' Franz said hopefully.

☻☻☻

Joseph Wright stood on the balcony of the lakeside villa, sipping from a tumbler of excellent whisky and listening to the sound of the waves washing against the shore. This particular safe house was one of his favourites, not least because absolutely no one knew of its existence. He knew that Nero would have correctly assumed that the attempt on his life in London had been arranged by him and he was damned if he was going to make it easy for Nero, or worse, Raven, to find him. He had to admit that the assassination attempt had been an act of desperation on his part. Like many of the former members of the ruling council he was determined that Nero was not going to strip him of all the power that he had managed to accrue over the years. He had hoped that if Nero could be taken out of the picture that the new ruling council would have disintegrated. Nero may have believed that a council made up of his own Alpha stream graduates would be fit to replace the departed leaders of G.L.O.V.E. but they all knew that it would only work if Nero was there to guide them. Without his hand on the rudder the ship would soon be drifting aimlessly and the old guard would once again be able to seize control. It was a nice theory at least but Wright knew that Nero would prove more difficult to dislodge with each passing day, while his own power and that of the other former members of the ruling council would only diminish with time.

The mobile phone on the glass table behind him began to ring, startling him from his brooding and Wright looked at the display. It read: CALLER UNKNOWN.

'Hello,' Wright said, putting the phone to his ear.

'Good evening, Mr Wright,' a digitally distorted voice on the other end replied.

'Who is this?' Wright demanded impatiently.

'My name is Minerva,' the voice replied, 'and I represent a group of people who would very much like to discuss the possibility of forming an alliance with you and the other members of your organisation who have been harmed by Maximilian Nero's clumsy grab for power.'

'Really,' Wright said, sounding sceptical, 'and who exactly might this group of people you represent be?'

'We are people who share a common interest in the destruction of Nero,' Minerva replied. 'I suspect you may have heard of us – we are called the Disciples.'

☻☻☻

'You OK?' Laura asked, as she looked up from the lines of code displayed on the device's screen and caught Otto staring off into the distance.

'Sorry, what?' Otto said, his eyes focusing on her.

'I asked if you were OK,' Laura said. 'You were miles away.'

'Yeah, sorry, I'm fine. It was just a bit weird to see Tom and Penny again,' Otto said with a sigh. 'It just seems so long ago, you know, life before this place. Sometimes I feel like I'm never going to see the real world again. That I'm never going to leave. Do you know what I mean?'

'Of course I do,' Laura said. 'I'm sure we all feel like that sometimes but there's going to be a life after H.I.V.E. you know. For all of us.'

91

'Assuming we survive till then,' Otto said with a wry smile.

'Well, there is that,' Laura said, 'although it's been several months since anyone tried to kill us so that has to be a good sign.'

'And yet here we are working on a device that will probably end up getting us killed. It'll either explode or Doctor Nero will catch us with it. Either way we're dead,' Otto said cheerily.

'I'll have you know that there's a remarkably low chance of this exploding,' Laura said with mock indignation. 'If you'd designed it on the other hand, well, then we might as well be playing hopscotch in a minefield.'

'Ouch, suppose I asked for that,' Otto said with a grin.

Laura stared at the lines of code on the display.

'Otto, can I ask you something?' Laura said after a few seconds, still staring at the screen.

'Sure, what's the matter?' Otto asked, sensing the change in her tone.

'Do you remember when we were in Brazil and you were still infected with the Animus fluid?' Laura said quietly.

'Bits of it,' Otto said. 'It's not something I particularly like to think about, to be honest.' The whole experience of being turned against his friends by Animus and then being nearly taken over by Overlord was not something that Otto was keen to relive.

'I know, I'm sorry, it's not fair of me to ask. Forget about it,' Laura said, shaking her head slightly.

'No, it's fine, it's in the past. What was it you wanted to ask?'

'You were really, really ill and you were starting to slip away and we all . . .' Laura paused for a moment and then looked him straight in the eye. 'We all thought you were going to die and just before you lost consciousness you whispered something to me. Do you remember what you said?'

'I . . . I'm not . . . yes,' Otto said, looking down at the floor. 'Yes, I remember.'

'I know you were delirious and it was probably because of that but . . . I need to know . . . did you mean what you said?'

Otto stared at her for several long seconds, trying to find the words he wanted.

'I . . .'

'Woah,' Shelby said as the door slid open and she saw Otto and Laura. 'Sorry . . . erm . . . wrong room. I'll . . . err . . . come back later.'

'No, it's all right,' Laura said, looking at Otto. 'I think we're finished here.'

Otto looked like he was going to say something and then he stood up.

'Are you sure, because I can go hit the books in the library if you guys still need some time to . . . er . . . debug,' Shelby said, looking questioningly at Laura.

'No, it's OK, the device is ready,' Laura said, picking it up and handing it to Otto. 'We're all going to need a good night's sleep if we're seriously going to pull this plan off tomorrow night.'

'Laura's right,' Otto said, slipping the device into his jumpsuit pocket. 'I should go. See you guys tomorrow.'

'You all right?' Shelby asked as the door hissed shut behind Otto.

'Yeah . . . no . . . oh, I don't know,' Laura said, sitting down on the edge of her bed.

'Want to talk about it?'

'No, not right now,' Laura said with a sigh. 'Not right now.'

☣☣☣

'You should have seen your face,' Penny said with a grin as the Alphas walked out of their Stealth and Evasion class.

'How was I supposed to know?' Tom asked, looking embarrassed. 'No one told me.'

'Well, at least now you'll always be remembered for something,' Otto said as he put his backpack on his shoulder, 'Tom Ransom. First H.I.V.E. student to actually stroke Ms Leon.'

'The look on your face when she asked you what you thought you were doing . . . priceless,' Laura chuckled.

Ms Leon was H.I.V.E.'s Stealth and Evasion teacher who, as a result of a freak accident involving one of Professor Pike's experiments, had found her consciousness transferred into the body of a cat. Unfortunately Tom had not realised that when he first encountered her.

'I've never actually heard an Alpha class all gasp at once like that before,' Shelby said. 'That's good going.'

'It's going to take me a while to live this one down, isn't it?' Tom moaned.

'It could have been worse,' Otto said. 'You could have given Colonel Francisco a neck rub.'

'Please not to be mentioning the Colonel,' Franz said with a sigh. 'Somehow he has been finding out that I was responsible for the toilet destruction incident and we all have a gym session this afternoon. I am already feeling the pain.'

'Oh great, a workout with an angry Francisco, just what my day needed,' Nigel said with a sigh. 'I don't suppose there's any chance he's going to have developed a passion for yoga, is there?'

'Not unless someone's developed some form of combat yoga,' Otto replied. 'Actually, you know, that might be quite cool. Fourteen ways to kill a man from the lotus position.'

'So what's our next lesson?' Penny asked as they all walked down the corridor.

'Holographic training session,' Laura replied. 'It's actually pretty cool. It's where they train us to do all the stuff that would be too dangerous or impractical to do for real. They're teaching us how to pilot helicopters at the moment.'

'Can I politely request that someone else be Otto's co-pilot this week,' Wing said with the tiniest hint of a smile. 'Last week's lesson was a little too . . . eventful for my tastes.'

'Hey!' Otto said. 'The landings are tough.'

'Yes,' Wing replied, 'but the rotor blades are supposed to be on top when you land, are they not?'

'Everyone's a critic,' Otto replied. 'OK, so I admit it wasn't perfect.'

'I believe that what the instructor actually said was . . . now let me get this right . . . instantly lethal to the crew and anyone standing within one hundred metres of the landing pad,' Wing said.

'I'm sure he said something about a fiery ball of exploding death too,' Laura said.

'Sounds like fun,' Tom said with a grin.

'Oh, you're going to fit right in around here,' Nigel sighed.

As Otto and the others arrived at the entrance to the holographic training cavern, the previous group of students were just leaving. Otto frowned slightly as he saw Cole Harrington walking straight towards him.

'Good to see you, Otto,' Harrington said as he approached. 'Have you got two minutes? There's something we need to discuss.'

Wing looked at Otto, raising an eyebrow quizzically.

'You guys go ahead,' Otto said. 'This won't take long.'

The other Alphas headed into the training area while Otto and Harrington waited for the corridor to clear.

'So, I was wondering if you'd had enough time to consider my offer from yesterday,' Harrington said with a cold smile.

'I don't know where you heard that I was the person to talk to about this,' Otto replied, 'but I don't have the exam papers and even if I did I wouldn't share them with you.'

'And that's your final decision,' Harrington said. 'There's nothing I can do to change your mind?'

'No,' Otto said, looking the other boy straight in the eye.

'That's a shame,' Harrington said, the smile disappearing. 'You're going to regret this. Trust me.'

'That's the second time you've threatened me,' Otto replied. 'You should know that I've been threatened by far more dangerous people than you. Do you know what none of those people have now?'

'What?'

'A pulse,' Otto said coldly.

'Is that supposed to frighten me?' Harrington said with a sneer.

'I don't know,' Otto replied, 'but I have heard that it's hard to scare people with low intelligence.'

'You're going to regret this,' Harrington said, his eyes narrowing, 'believe me. You Alphas are all the same – you think you're in control but you're not.'

'I don't care who's in control,' Otto said calmly before turning and heading into the training cavern. 'Just as long as it isn't someone like you.'

☻ ☻ ☻

The limousine drove between the warehouses, slowing to a halt outside the final set of rolling shutters. The driver sounded the horn once and as the metal shutters rolled upwards he pulled inside, parking in the middle of the loading bay. Moments after the shutters hit the ground the floor beneath the limo began to drop into a concealed shaft below. After a minute or so the hidden lift came to a stop and another set of gates in the wall of the shaft opened up, allowing the car access to the parking area on the other side, which was already half full with equally expensive vehicles. The chauffeur stepped out of the car and opened the rear door for the single passenger within. Joseph Wright stepped out and walked quickly towards the armoured double doors on the far side of the garage. He placed his hand in the recess next to the door and felt a tiny prick in one of his fingertips as a drop of his blood was extracted.

'DNA scan complete,' a digitised voice said after a few seconds. 'Access granted. Good evening, Mr Wright.'

The heavy doors rumbled open and Wright walked inside. The room was already filled with the hushed muttering of several subdued conversations that were taking place between the dozen men and women already present.

'Ladies and gentlemen,' Wright said, after looking round the room, 'please take your seats. Everyone seems to be here and we have much to discuss.'

The various men and women sat round the large conference table that occupied the centre of the room.

'First I would like to thank you all for coming,' Wright said. 'I know that things have been somewhat chaotic over the past few months but I believe that now is the time to put that behind us and focus instead on the future.'

'Get on with it, Wright,' Luca Venturi, the former head of G.L.O.V.E.'s Southern European operations said impatiently. 'I don't know about anyone else but I have an organisation to try and rebuild and I really don't have time for this. I'm sure everyone heard about your bungled attempt on Nero's life. I'm not surprised that you would rather focus on the future when the past is littered with failure.'

'You talk of rebuilding, Luca. Well, that is exactly why I asked all of you here tonight,' Wright replied quickly. 'We've all suffered as a result of Maximilian Nero's decision to disband G.L.O.V.E.'s ruling council. We have all watched as the criminal empires that we each worked for decades to build were undermined by the actions of just one man. We were thrown to the wolves, left to fend for ourselves as the organisation that we built was stolen from us by Nero and his lackeys. Well, starting tonight I propose that we pool our resources and begin the battle to take back what is rightfully ours. Are we really going to stand by while Nero appoints a new council entirely made up of former pupils of that damned school of his? People who have not earned the positions to which they have been appointed. Nero and his council are weak – the time to strike is now.'

'I hate to break it to you, Jospeh,' Felicia Diaz, one-time commander of G.L.O.V.E.'s operations in South America, said with a sigh, 'but even if we were all to work together, we would still not have the resources to take on Nero. He still controls G.L.O.V.E. and you know as well as I do that the loyalties of the organisation's members are commanded by one thing . . . strength. Once upon a time people may have respected our strength but now they know what the true balance of power is. The new ruling council that Nero has assembled may be inexperienced but as long as Nero sits at the head of the table the people who report in to the council members will follow their instructions. No one wants to meet the same fate that befell Carlos, waking up one morning to find a walking, talking death sentence standing at the end of your bed.' There was a murmur of agreement round the table as the former members of the council recalled the grim fate that had met Carlos Chavez, Diaz's predecessor, when he had betrayed Nero.

'I think it's safe to assume we would all rather avoid an encounter with Nero's pet assassin but I did not gather us here this evening for nothing. I believe that there may be a way to shift the balance of power. I have been approached by an organisation that would like to assist us in regaining control of G.L.O.V.E., an organisation that has both the resources we require and the willingness to use them.'

Wright reached inside his jacket and pulled out a small disc-shaped device, placing it in the centre of the table. A moment later the disc lit up with a bright white light and a holographic image of a digitally distorted face appeared hovering in the air half a metre above it.

'Good evening, ladies and gentlemen,' the hovering face said, its voice also electronically disguised. 'My name is Minerva and I represent an organisation that some of you will already be familiar with. We are called the Disciples and we would like to offer you our assistance in over-throwing Maximilian Nero and restoring control of G.L.O.V.E. to its rightful masters. You.'

'Are you insane, Wright?' Luca Venturi asked, clear astonishment in his voice. 'These people were the servants of Overlord. I may disagree with what Nero has done but these lunatics were intent on handing the world over to an insane, genocidal artificial intelligence. What on earth makes you think that we can trust them?'

'Overlord is dead,' Minerva said calmly, 'and with his destruction came a change in the priorities of our organisation. There were many of us that did not agree with what Overlord had planned and saw him as merely a means to an end. We saw beyond the destruction that Overlord would have wrought and sensed the opportunity to change things permanently. Nero wishes the forces of global villainy to remain hidden in the shadows, frightened to show our true power for fear of inviting the retribution of the world's governments. Why? What does that achieve? When will we finally be allowed to show the world what we are truly capable of and take the reigns of global power for ourselves? We are tired of hiding. The time has come to step out of the shadows and seize the power that is rightfully yours. However, to achieve that power we must work together. You need our resources and we need allies but, more than that, we need leadership. That is why we are turning to you. Our assets, both human and financial, are considerable, but we lack the networks and contacts that you have built up in your many years of service to G.L.O.V.E. There is a unique opportunity now for us to pool our resources and create a new organisation that will not suffer from the frightened paralysis that Nero favours. G.L.O.V.E. was designed to stop you from achieving your true potential and that is why it must be swept away and replaced with an organisation that is not paralysed by fear but will instead rule *through* fear.'

'Fine words,' Felicia Diaz said, staring at the holographic projection, 'but why should we trust you when you will not even show us your true face?'

'What difference would that make?' Minerva replied. 'Surely the only thing that would really prove to you that you can trust us is if we give you a meaningful demonstration of what we are willing to do for you.'

'Such as?' Diaz asked.

'Such as the destruction of Nero,' Minerva said calmly.

'Many have tried to kill Maximilian,' Luca Venturi snorted. 'Obviously, all have failed. What makes you think you will be any more successful?'

'I didn't say we would kill him,' Minerva replied. 'I said we would destroy him. If we were to assassinate him, one of his acolytes would simply step forward and take his place. Certainly G.L.O.V.E. would be weakened but not to the degree that we need. So, instead, we must make sure that he is crippled so completely that it will paralyse G.L.O.V.E. permanently. That is when we will strike and replace them once and for all. By the time we are finished Nero will not be dead – he will just wish he was.'

chapter six

'You sure we can trust them?' Shelby asked.

'As sure as I can be,' Otto replied. He leant on the balcony railing, looking down at the atrium area of accommodation block seven where Tom and Penny were chatting with Nigel and Franz. 'I know you guys only met them yesterday but I've known them for a lot longer. Besides, it's not like we're asking them to do anything really difficult – they'll just be backing up Nigel and Franz. We could with a couple more pairs of hands for that part of the operation anyway.'

'Should we not be more concerned with whether or not they will wish to take part in such a risky venture at all?' Wing asked. 'They have, after all, only just arrived.'

'I don't think they'll mind,' Otto said with a smile. 'It sounds like they were quite used to taking a few risks in their lives before they were brought here. Besides, as I recall there was a certain bunch of newly recruited students who hatched a plan to escape from H.I.V.E. within just a couple of weeks of arriving. Let me think, who was that?'

'Point taken,' Wing replied.

'I'm with Otto,' Laura said with a nod. 'Even if they don't want to get involved I'm pretty sure that we can trust them not to tell anyone what we're up to.'

'Sounds like we're agreed,' Shelby said, looking at the other three. 'Who's going to brief them?'

'I'll do it,' Otto said. 'It might sound a little less crazy coming from someone they've known for more than twenty-four hours. I'll fill them in on the details – you guys make sure that you've got everything else we need. We go at midnight.'

Wing, Shelby and Laura all nodded their agreement and headed back to their quarters to make their final preparations. Otto walked down the stairs at the end of the landing and across the atrium towards where Tom and Penny were sitting with Franz and Nigel.

'Hey guys,' Otto said as he approached, 'how's it going?'

'Fine, thanks,' Penny replied. 'Franz was just telling us how he single-handedly saved the school when it was taken over by an army of robot assassins.'

'Whether we like it or not,' Nigel said, rolling his eyes.

'I am, of course, usually being reluctant to talk of my

heroic actions,' Franz said with a dismissive wave, 'but Tom and Penny are insisting that I give them all the details.'

'Of course they were,' Otto said, trying not to laugh at the slightly strained smiles on the new Alphas' faces. 'Hey, I was just wondering if I could have a word with Tom and Penny in private.'

'Sure, no problem,' Nigel said. 'We were just going to head up to our quarters anyway.'

'Yes, we are needing to get ready for a good night's sleep,' Franz said, just slightly too loudly and with a painfully obvious wink at Otto.

'You do that,' Otto said.

'We will NOT be seeing you later,' Franz said as Nigel dragged him away.

'Is Franz always so . . . erm . . . .?' Penny asked as Otto sat down.

'Yes, always,' Otto replied with a small sigh. 'Don't worry, you get used to it . . . eventually.'

'What can we do for you?' Tom asked.

'Well,' Otto replied, 'there's something that a few of us have been planning for a while and we were wondering if you two might want to be involved.'

'What kind of something?' Penny asked.

'The kind of something that I think might appeal to you guys,' Otto replied with a smile.

'OK, I'm intrigued,' Tom said, leaning forward. 'Tell me more.'

Otto spent the next ten minutes describing exactly what it was that he and the others had planned for later that night.

'That's insane,' Penny said as Otto finished. 'I love it! I'm in.'

'Me too,' Tom said with a grin. 'You know, I think I'm going to like it here.'

☢ ☢ ☢

Nero walked into the conference room and was pleased to see that the other members of G.L.O.V.E.'s new ruling council had already arrived. Perhaps *arrived* wasn't quite the right word since none of them were there in person. They were just three-dimensional projections created by the holographic display unit mounted in the ceiling above the centre of the long table, but this was as close as they could get to meeting in the flesh at short notice. As ever, Nero would have preferred to have gathered them all in person but for now this would have to do.

'Good evening, ladies and gentlemen,' Nero said as he took his seat at the head of the table. 'I will be brief as I know that you all have other pressing matters to attend to. It cannot have escaped your notice that there are two vacant seats at this table tonight. As I'm sure you are aware this is a result of actions by at least one former member of this council. Over the past few hours something even more troubling has come to my attention. I received a message from an old and trusted ally of this council and I have asked you all here so that he can share the same information with you.' Nero pressed a button on the control panel mounted in the table in front of him and the large display screen at the other end of the room lit up with a familiar face. 'Please go ahead, Diabolus.'

'Thank you, Max,' Diabolus Darkdoom replied with a nod. 'As some of you may know, I have been working over the past few months to find out more about the group known as the Disciples. At first it was difficult to discover anything more than the rumours and misinformation that we were already aware of. What we did know was that they were followers of Overlord and appeared to have a wide-spread and capable network of operatives. Initially I had hoped that the reason it was proving so difficult to discover anything was that their organisation had collapsed after the destruction of Overlord at the Advanced Weapons Project facility in Colorado. Gradually it became clear that this was, unfortunately, not the case. The Disciples had not been destroyed, they were merely regrouping. The first unpleasant evidence of this was the disappearance of several informants who had been providing us with information to track down the remaining members of the group. Soon after that other more subtle but equally disturbing signs began to emerge. I uncovered evidence of a marked increase in global weapons thefts and black market sales. We're not talking about a few shipping containers of AK-47s here. These were bleeding edge weapons systems and tactical equipment. The sort of stuff that some of the world's most powerful nations would be pleased to get their hands on and yet nobody seems to know where they've gone.'

'Are we sure that the Disciples are responsible?' one of the members of the council asked.

'It's impossible to be sure but we are aware of no other group with either the will or the resources to pull off these kinds of operations. Other than ourselves, of course. Within the past twenty-four hours things have taken a more sinister turn. As you all know, most of the former members of this council were less than happy with Doctor Nero's decision to dismiss them and assemble a new council. After the events surrounding Overlord's defeat they were forced into hiding. Overlord had, after all, revealed all of their identities to the world's security services. Despite that, Doctor Nero and myself had worked hard to keep tabs on their whereabouts and activities. They are too dangerous for us not to. The reason I am here talking to you today is that since last night they have also disappeared. We have lost contact with the operatives who were tracking them and the few members of the previous council who were sympathetic to Doctor Nero's decision have been assassinated. At exactly the same time we lost all contact with the G.L.O.V.E. operatives who had been assigned to further investigate the Disciples. It is highly unlikely that this was a coincidence. The conclusion we have been forced to draw is that the former members of the council may have allied themselves with the Disciples. While I have no direct evidence of it, every instinct is telling me that they are preparing for something big and that we are clearly the most likely targets.'

'Thank you, Diabolus,' Nero said, looking round the table. 'This is worrying but not entirely unexpected. What concerns me far more is their potential alliance with the Disciples – a group of people who were assisting Overlord in his insane plans, who would have stood by and watched as the whole world burned.'

'So how do we react?' another council member asked. 'How do we fight an enemy we can't find?'

'We can't,' Nero replied, shaking his head. 'We can only bolster our defences and wait for them to make their move. Normally I would be reluctant to take such a passive approach but until we have better intelligence on what we are up against I'm afraid that we have little choice.'

'I assume that our efforts to locate the missing former council members are still ongoing?' someone else asked.

'Indeed,' Nero replied. 'We are using every means at our disposal to relocate them and when we do they will face . . .

vigorous questioning. I will see to that personally. In the meantime you should all make a special effort to watch for any unusual activity in your own territories. The Disciples will have to break cover at some point and when they do we will be waiting for them. Thank you for your time. Do unto others.'

'Do unto others,' the members of the ruling council repeated the G.L.O.V.E. motto as the holographic projector deactivated and they faded from view.

'Is there anything else you need, Max?' Darkdoom asked, seeing the concern in his friend's expression.

'No,' Nero said with a sigh. 'You can see where this is heading, I assume.'

'This isn't a war yet,' Darkdoom replied. 'We can still defuse this situation before it comes to that.'

'I hope you're right, Diabolus,' Nero said, shaking his head. 'I really do.'

☻☻☻

'One minute,' Otto said, looking at the timer on his Blackbox as Wing checked the contents of his backpack for the final time.

'I would wish us good luck but I know you do not approve of such things,' Wing said, smiling.

'If success is dictated by luck, then it isn't really success at all,' Otto replied, still staring at his Blackbox.

'So you have said many times,' Wing said, raising an eyebrow, 'but I would still rather have it than not.'

'Having said that, Franz does play a significant part in this plan so maybe a little bit of luck actually wouldn't hurt.'

'Personally, I think that it is good that Franz is so keen to be involved. He has been most . . . enthusiastic.'

'You say enthusiastic; I say like a really, really excited puppy in that split second before it pees on you.'

'Thank you, Otto,' Wing frowned, 'for putting a calming mental image in my head just moments before we are to embark on such a perilous enterprise.'

'All part of the service,' Otto said with a grin as his Blackbox emitted a single soft beep. 'OK, it's time.'

Wing hit the light switch, plunging the room into darkness as Otto picked up the device that he and Laura had secretly been working on for the last couple of weeks. Once upon a time it had been a Blackbox belonging to Colonel Francisco that Shelby had 'borrowed', but now it was barely recognisable. Just about the only thing that remained the same was the high-resolution touch-screen display. The rest of the device was covered in wiring and pieces of exposed circuit board. Otto and Laura had even given it a new nickname, the Hackbox. Otto touched a command on the screen and it began to display a series of status messages.

SECURE COMMUNICATIONS PROTOCOL ESTABLISHED
MOBILE NETWORK ESTABLISHED
CONNECTING TO SLAVE DEVICES
MALPENSE, O CONNECTED
BRAND, L CONNECTED
FANCHU, W CONNECTED
TRINITY, S CONNECTED
DARKDOOM, N CONNECTED
ARGENTBLUM, F CONNECTED
RANSOM, T CONNECTED
RICHARDS, P CONNECTED
ALL SLAVE DEVICES SUCCESSFULLY CONNECTED
SURVEILLANCE LOOP ACTIVATED
OPENING ACCOMMODATION BLOCK 7 DOORS 23, 38, 42, 72
    AND 75.

The door to Otto and Wing's room hissed open.

'Come on,' Otto said as he hurried out of their quarters.

They ran down the landing and met Shelby and Laura coming the other way.

'So far so good,' Shelby whispered.

'If you mean that we've just successfully passed the first of four hundred and seventy-three separate potential failure points in this plan, then yeah, so far so good,' Otto replied.

'Thanks for the morale boost, Roboto,' Shelby said.

'Hush up, you two,' Laura sighed. 'I'm as much of a fan of snarky banter as the next girl but we've only got an hour until the surveillance loop expires. Come on.'

They hurried along the landing to Franz and Nigel's room where they found only Nigel waiting.

'Where's Franz?' Otto asked with a frown.

'He's "scouting ahead" apparently,' Nigel said, shaking his head. 'I told him to wait here but he said, and I quote, "That danger lurks round every corner and that he was on point".'

'Oh no,' Otto cringed. 'Really?'

'Don't blame me,' Nigel said. 'I wasn't the one at the planning meeting who told him to "channel his inner ninja".'

'I was only kidding,' Shelby said defensively.

'OK, let's get Tom and Penny and round Franz up before he attacks any security guards,' Otto sighed.

They all hurried down the stairs to the next landing where Tom and Penny were waiting.

'You managed to get out without waking up your new room-mates then?'

'Yeah,' Penny replied, 'though I think it might have had something to do with the sedative drops on their pillows. You sure that one drop will be enough to keep them under?'

'Should be more than enough,' Otto replied, as they continued down the stairs to the atrium. We're not going to be gone that long.'

'Where exactly did you get that stuff from anyway?' Laura asked.

'It was something that I'd been ... working on,' Otto replied slightly uncomfortably.

'Why were you working on a new form of sedative?' Nigel asked.

'It wasn't really supposed to be a sedative, it was just supposed to relax the airways and ... erm ... control snoring.'

'Otto, is there something you would like to tell me?' Wing said with a slight frown.

'Look, there's Franz,' Otto said quickly.

Franz was dashing from shadow to shadow, slowly making his way towards the huge steel doors that sealed off the accommodation block at night.

'What's he got on his face?' Shelby asked.

'Don't ask,' Nigel said.

As they approached they could all see that Franz's entire face was black.

'Franz, what have you done?' Laura asked, stifling a giggle.

'I am ensuring that I am blending with the shadows,' Franz said. 'It is increasing my stealthiness.'

'What did you use?' Otto asked, staring at him in mild disbelief.

'I am using the marker pen but I am being very careful

not to get any in my mouth because the label on the pen is saying that it is inedible,' Franz said with a serious expression.

'Indelible, Franz, indelible,' Otto said.

'Oh no,' Nigel said, putting his hand over his eyes.

'What is this indelible meaning?' Franz said as he noticed the mixture of amusement and horror on the other Alphas' faces.

'Never mind,' Otto said. 'We'll deal with it later. We need to keep moving. Laura, get the door.' Otto handed the Hackbox to Laura and she walked over to the numeric keypad that served as a lock for the massive door. She touched a series of buttons on the device's screen and a couple of seconds later the doors began to slowly rumble apart.

'OK, no alarms going off, so I'm going to assume that the ghost interface is working,' Laura said.

'I never doubted you for a moment,' Otto said, smiling at Laura. 'Right. Everyone knows where they need to be. We have . . .' Otto looked at his Blackbox, 'fifty-three minutes. Good luck.'

Otto, Wing, Laura and Shelby jogged away down the corridor ahead while Nigel and Franz headed off down another corridor with Tom and Penny. Otto reached out with his mind and his own strange ability to control electronic devices allowed him to hook up directly to the Hackbox. It was safe for him to connect with it as long as

116

he didn't go a stage further and connect directly to H.I.V.E.'s network.

'Right, give me a second,' Otto said, as he visualised a three-dimensional image of the layout of H.I.V.E., 'let's see what we can see.' On the map in Otto's head, small points of moving light began to appear. There were bright blue dots that represented the locations of his friends' Blackboxes and a scattering of red dots throughout the complex that showed the current positions of the security patrols. He tilted his head to one side slightly and sent a live feed of that information to the Hackbox which then passed it on to the other Blackboxes.

'Got it,' Laura said, checking the screen of her own device. 'The Hackbox is transmitting.'

'OK, that should help us avoid any patrols,' Otto said. 'Now we just need some new outfits.'

The four of them ran through the twisting maze of corridors, stopping only briefly to let security patrols pass by ahead of them. They quickly made their way deeper into the bowels of the volcano that housed the school. The lower levels were more dimly lit, with uniform grey concrete walls and floors.

'It'd be real easy to get lost down here,' Shelby said as they ran down yet another featureless corridor.

'Don't worry, we're nearly there,' Laura said, looking at the Hackbox. 'Next left.'

They took the next branch in the tunnel and the corridor ended at a steel door with the words 'Storage Area Four' etched into its surface.

'Right, here we are,' Otto said. 'Open sesame.'

Laura tapped at the Hackbox and the door slid open. As the four of them stepped into the storage area, lights started to flicker on overhead.

'Woah,' Laura said, pointing at the opposite wall, 'are they what I think they are?'

Standing against the wall were three of the hulking assault droids that Cypher had used in his assault on H.I.V.E. a couple of years before.

'I had wondered if they'd kept any of these,' Otto said as he examined one of the giant machines more closely. 'Do you think they're still functional?'

'I suppose it would depend on the condition of the servos and the musculature interlinks,' Laura replied, tracing her finger through the dust that covered one of the huge machines.

'Tick tock, guys,' Shelby said as she looked around the room. 'We need to stay on schedule. Anybody see what we're here for?'

'Over here,' Wing said, beckoning the others.

Hanging on a rack were a dozen thermoptic camouflage bodysuits.

'Get changed,' Otto said. 'The other four should be in position any minute.'

'I'm having a bit of trouble here,' Laura said, frowning at the display on the Hackbox.

'What is it?' Otto asked.

'They need to get closer to the door to the CPC or else I can't get a link to the locking mechanism from their Blackboxes,' Laura said.

Otto looked at the display of his own Blackbox. The security patrols around that area were tight. Nigel and the others had a window of forty-five seconds, a minute at the outside, before another patrol arrived. He watched as the dots on the display representing their friends moved closer to their target.

'Laura,' Otto said, frowning, 'they need that door open now.'

'I know, I know,' Laura said, chewing her bottom lip nervously.

☢ ☢ ☢

'Wait,' Nigel whispered to Franz, Tom and Penny, holding up his hand. At the far end of the corridor a pair of security guards walked past. Nigel waited, studying the display of his Blackbox. 'Go,' he said and the four of them hurried down the corridor. Ahead was a large double door that looked like it would be more at home in a bank vault. 'OK,' Nigel said, 'let's hope this works.'

'It had better,' Tom said, placing a hand on the massive

door, 'because we're not getting through these doors any other way. Not without enough explosives to bring this whole place down around our ears anyway.'

Nigel looked nervously at his Blackbox. There was another security patrol heading their way. They only had a few more seconds.

'Come on, guys,' Nigel muttered to himself.

Suddenly the thick steel rods that crossed the door slid back and they began to open. Nigel and the others hurried through the gap and almost immediately the doors began to close again. Nigel watched the position of the security patrol on his Blackbox, praying that the doors would shut and lock before the patrol came round the corner outside. All four of them held their breaths as the red dot moved down the corridor on the screen, followed by a collective sigh of relief as the guards continued along their assigned patrol route.

'Thank you, Laura,' Nigel said, 'even if you did cut it a little close.' He thumbed the comms button on his Blackbox and a second later Otto connected.

'We're in,' Nigel said. 'Over to you.'

'Roger that,' Otto replied. 'See you on the other side.'

Nigel turned round and tried to take in the scale of the room they were standing in. Six massive circular turbines, each several storeys high and thrumming with power, took up the majority of the floor. Surrounding the turbines were huge towers with giant metal balls on top of them that discharged arcing bolts of man-made lightning from one to another. The room was only dimly lit and the flashes of bright blue-white light from the thunderous electrical discharges threw odd shadows on to the walls. This was the Central Power Core, where the heat gathered by the school's geothermal plant was converted into raw power that was then distributed throughout H.I.V.E. If H.I.V.E.mind was the school's brain, then this place was its beating heart.

'OK, Penny, you come with me to the control room. You two go down to the main floor and get ready by those breakers. Remember that you have to trip them at the precise moment I say or Otto and the others are going to have a really unpleasant evening.'

'You can be counting on us,' Franz said, giving Nigel a thumbs up before climbing down the ladder to the generator floor.

Nigel and Penny ran along the gantry accessway to the elevated control room on the other side of the chamber.

'If this place is so important, why is there nobody here?' Penny asked as they entered the deserted control room.

'It's all fully automated,' Nigel replied, searching for the right controls. 'H.I.V.E.mind runs it all. The manual controls are only here in case the computer systems go down for any reason. At least that's what Otto told me.'

Nigel found the correct panel and quickly identified the controls that Otto and Laura had briefed him on.

'Are you guys in position?' Nigel said, speaking into his Blackbox.

'Ready,' Tom replied after a moment.

'I am being ready too,' Franz said.

'OK,' Nigel replied, 'now we wait for Otto's signal.'

☻☻☻

Otto lay on his belly inside the ventilation shaft, looking down through the grille into the room below. He was suddenly very glad that he didn't suffer from vertigo – the floor was a good fifty metres below them. He reached over his shoulder and unzipped the side pocket of his backpack, pulling out a small steel multi-tool. He unfolded a screw-driver blade from the tool and set to work quickly unscrewing the mountings that held the grille in place. He pulled the loose grille free and handed it back to Wing. There was an ominous creaking sound from somewhere overhead.

'You are sure this shaft is strong enough to support us all, aren't you, Otto?' Laura whispered from somewhere behind Wing.

'Define sure,' Otto said, sliding forward and popping his head through the hole in the floor of the shaft.

'Oh, great,' Laura sighed.

Otto scanned the room beneath them. This was

H.I.V.E.mind's primary data hub and as such was one of the most sensitive and well-secured locations in the entire school. Thick translucent cables pulsing with blue light led down from the ceiling in the centre of the brightly lit room and into a central column. Beneath the hub more cables led down to the floor far below and fanned out to an array of black monoliths arranged in concentric circles. These black slabs were H.I.V.E.mind's storage cores and inside one of them was the data that they wanted. There was just one small catch. A metre above the tops of the storage cores was what, from Otto's position far above, looked like a sheet of sparkling blue light. It was actually quite beautiful, a fact which concealed its true purpose. What it actually was, Otto had discovered during the planning of the operation, was a fine mesh of high-powered argon lasers that would instantly vaporise anything that touched it. Its main purpose was to stop anything that fell from above damaging the precious storage cores but it also served as a highly effective security system. That wasn't the only problem. Positioned at regular intervals just above the gantry that ran round the circular walls of the room were a dozen sentry devices with mounted Sleeper pulse guns. They would track the thermal signature of anyone entering the hub without the proper clearance and neutralise them. The fact that the entire room was chilled to just above freezing point in order to keep the hub's processors cool would make any such thermal signatures incredibly easy to spot. It was figuring out how to get past these systems, and not Wing's snoring, that had kept Otto awake at night.

'OK, Laura,' Otto said, 'signal Nigel once we're in position. Wing, Shel, fire up your suits. Time to go.'

Otto pointed the grappler unit mounted on the forearm of his suit at the top of the ventilation shaft above the opening and fired. The metal dart punched through the thin wall of the shaft and clamped on. Otto activated his thermoptic camouflage system and carefully slid forward, lowering himself into the opening. The heads-up display in his mask started a five-minute countdown. The suits that they'd borrowed from the storage room were obsolete, first-generation units which meant that they only had enough battery power to run the camouflage systems for five minutes at a time. While they were active Otto, Wing and Shelby would be effectively invisible not only to the naked eye but also to the thermal sensors on the sentry guns. None of them wanted to still be in this room when that countdown expired. The incredibly thin line spooled out from the grappler unit as Otto descended towards the glittering blue laser field. Above him, first Wing and then Shelby dropped through the opening and began their own careful descents. Otto slowed his descent and pointed the grappler on his other arm at the gantry that led to the column in the centre of the room. He fired a second line and slowly reeled himself over towards the gantry. He caught hold of the railing and climbed over on to the walkway leading to the central hub before releasing and retracting his two grappler lines. He hurried over to one of the control panels mounted in the column and pulled a metal box with a small aerial from his backpack.

Above them, Laura watched as her friends moved into position. The computer-assisted optics in the helmet of her own suit allowed her to see them despite the fact that they were currently invisible to the naked eye. Once Otto was all set and Wing and Shelby were positioned just above the laser net, she hit the button on her Blackbox to signal Nigel.

'Go ahead,' Nigel replied on the other end.

'We're ready,' Laura said quickly. 'Time to turn out the lights.'

�335 �335 �335

In the Power Core cavern Nigel hit the series of switches as Laura and Otto had drilled him. It would have been much simpler to just cut the power supply to the entire school but that would have been too obvious. This would be the first place that the security teams would be dispatched to and without power the four of them would be trapped inside this chamber just waiting for the guards to turn up. They had to be subtler than that.

'OK, Penny,' Nigel said, 'when I say, throw that switch.'

Penny nodded and placed her hand on the bright red switch in the centre of the console on the opposite side of the room. Nigel placed his Blackbox on the control panel and used it to signal Franz and Tom.

'OK, guys, here we go,' Nigel said, his hand hovering over a green button. 'Three, two, one, now!'

☉☉☉

H.I.V.E.mind knew something was wrong. All of the system diagnostics that he had run had come back clear. None of H.I.V.E.'s security systems were reporting anything strange but he could not shake off the feeling that there was something he was missing. If he were human he would probably have called it a hunch but, as he found he was having to remind himself more and more frequently, he was not human. Once upon a time he would have relied upon the simple facts that the diagnostics were reporting to him but ever since he had shared consciousnesses with Otto he had found himself more prone to this erratic behaviour. He floated through the data structures of the school, searching for the files he wanted. He quickly found the correct location and began to stream the raw footage from the school's surveillance network. All was as it should be, the only signs of life were the security guards conducting their regular patrols. H.I.V.E.mind froze the image of one of the guards walking past. There was something about it that was not quite right. He was just beginning to study the image in higher definition when suddenly everything went black.

☢ ☢ ☢

'There it goes,' Laura said as the automated signal, alerting security that H.I.V.E.mind was down, flashed across H.I.V.E.'s network. She watched as the Hackbox intercepted the signal and deleted it. They didn't have long – the majority of H.I.V.E.'s systems would automatically switch to the school's lower-level computer systems but sooner or later someone would make a direct enquiry to H.I.V.E.mind and then they would have only minutes before they figured out what had happened.

'Nigel, H.I.V.E.mind's down,' Laura said into her Blackbox. 'Cut the power to the laser net.'

In the chamber below the lethal blue field flickered for an instant and then vanished. Shelby and Wing dropped to the floor and reeled in their grappler lines. On the gantry above them Otto closed his eyes and placed a hand on the control panel mounted in the central column and reached out with his abilities for the storage cores below. Inside his head he flew through the vast fields of data that were stored in the black monoliths. Under other circumstances he would have taken this opportunity to delve deep into the secrets of H.I.V.E. but they didn't have time for that now. Now he had to find the maintenance controls for the storage units. He raced through the network, scanning the control systems at an inhuman speed until he found what he was looking for. The instant that H.I.V.E.mind was shut down he would have performed an emergency core dump. Everything that was in his active memory at that instant would have been copied to secure physical storage somewhere in this room. Otto accessed the maintenance controls and opened the core containing the correct drive.

'It's open,' Otto yelled from the gantry. 'Wing, Shelby, get going.'

Wing and Shelby ran in opposite directions, scanning the surfaces of the dozens of jet black slabs for the storage unit. Up on the gantry Otto watched the battery timer in his HUD drop below three minutes.

'Come on, guys,' Otto muttered under his breath. 'It's got to be down there somewhere.'

Shelby sprinted past the monoliths, looking for anything unusual. Suddenly something caught her eye. Protruding slightly from the surface of one of the slabs was a smaller black cube.

'Got it!' Shelby yelled, sliding the cube fully out of the slab and shoving it into her pocket. She looked upwards and aligned the laser sight on her grappler with the opening in the ventilation shaft far overhead and fired. The dart rocketed upwards, trailing its monofilament cable, and struck home, securing itself within the ventilation shaft. Shelby shot upwards off the floor, flying past the gantry where Otto was standing and up into the ventilation shaft.

'Present for you,' Shelby said with a grin, handing Laura the black cube as she climbed inside the shaft.

'Great,' Laura said. 'This won't take long.' She attached a series of self-adhesive pads to the surface of the cube and hooked them up to cables dangling from the back of the Hackbox.

'I still don't understand why we don't just get Otto to do that with his electronic voodoo,' Shelby said as she watched Laura urgently punching commands into the Hackbox.

'Because he'd leave digital fingerprints all over it,' Laura replied, staring at the tiny display. 'The moment that H.I.V.E.mind is brought back online he'll be restored from the data in this cube. He'd know instantly if Otto had accessed it. Don't ask me why, I don't really understand it myself, but Otto assures me that H.I.V.E.mind would know. It's something to do with this bond they've developed.'

'They do make a lovely couple,' Shelby said with a grin. 'I've always said they were made for each other.'

'Transfer complete!' Laura yelped delightedly. She handed the cube back to Shelby who turned and looked down through the opening in the shaft. Directly beneath them on the chamber floor far below Wing stood waiting.

'OK, big guy,' Shelby said, 'heads up.'

She dropped the cube through the opening and it plummeted towards Wing. Wing watched as it tumbled towards him, totally focused. He caught the cube in a single fluid motion that ensured it was not jarred by the sudden deceleration and ran back towards the storage core that Shelby had taken it from barely thirty seconds before. He slid the cube back into the monolith but it did not insert fully, the rest was up to Otto. On the gantry above Otto closed his eyes again and accessed the storage maintenance controls. The cube slid smoothly back into the black slab and Otto deleted the maintenance log that recorded the fact it had ever been removed. Otto opened his eyes and smiled – the countdown in his HUD showed a minute remaining on the camouflage system's battery. More than enough time for them to get out.

'OK, Wing, we're good. Let's go!' Otto yelled down to his friend. He aimed his grappler at the opening overhead and fired, reeling himself in the moment the dart hit home. He looked down as he climbed into the opening and saw Wing aim his grappler up at them. He fired and the dart shot past Otto and into the shaft wall. A split second later, in the instant before Wing could start his ascent, the laser net lit up again with a flash, severing Wing's grappler line instantly and trapping him beneath its lethal glow.

'No! Damn it,' Otto snapped, 'what happened? Laura, signal Nigel and tell him to cut the power again.'

Otto watched as the countdown in his HUD dropped below forty-five seconds.

'OK,' he said, looking at the girls, 'I think we have a problem.'

chapter seven

'Step away from the switch,' the security guard said, his Sleeper pointing straight at Tom.

Nigel and Penny watched in horror from the control room above as Tom stepped away from the circuit-breaker which the guard had just forced him to reset.

'What do we do?' Penny whispered.

'I have no idea,' Nigel replied. 'We just have to pray that the others got out in time.'

At that instant an incoming transmission request from Laura flashed up on Nigel's Blackbox and he hit the receive button.

'Nigel,' Laura said quickly, 'what's going on? The laser net just reactivated with Wing on the wrong side of it.'

'We've got a big problem here,' Nigel explained. 'A guard's just come in and caught Tom. The guard forced him to reset the circuit-breaker. There's nothing we can do.'

'Weren't you watching the patrols?' Laura asked irritably.

'I was,' Nigel moaned, 'but then I had to throw all those switches and I got distracted. I'm really sorry – I should have been paying more attention.'

'It doesn't matter,' Laura replied, 'we just need to get the grid turned off.'

Down on the floor of the Power Core, the guard reached for the radio attached to his belt.

'I'm going to call this in,' the guard said. 'Don't move a muscle unless you want to spend the next few hours unconscious.'

The guard hit the transmit button on the walkie-talkie.

'This is Evans in the CPC. I've got a . . .'

The guard's eyes widened in horror as a screaming, black-faced demon leapt from the shadows and hit him like a truck. He collapsed backwards under Franz's weight and as he landed flat on his back there was a muffled zap sound as his Sleeper discharged. Franz rolled off the unfortunate guard who had just accidentally rendered himself unconscious with his own weapon.

'Be throwing the switch,' Franz said as he climbed to his feet. 'Quickly.'

Tom blinked once in astonishment before rushing over to the circuit-breaker and throwing it back into the off position.

Up in the control room Nigel grinned at Penny.

'You know, we are *never* going to hear the end of this.'

☣ ☣ ☣

'Come on, guys,' Otto said under his breath as he looked down through the opening in the ventilation shaft. The battery counter on his HUD ticked below ten seconds. Wing had exactly the same charge remaining and the moment the batteries failed and the thermoptic camouflage disengaged he would be easy prey for the sentry guns on the walls. Otto did not like to think what the consequences would be if Nero realised what they had been doing. He watched the counter, feeling helpless.

Five . . .

Four . . .

Three . . .

Suddenly, the glittering laser net above Wing's head vanished. Wing reacted instantly, aiming the grappler on his other forearm at the small opening far overhead. Otto scooted back from the opening as the grappler bolt struck the ceiling of the shaft. The battery timer hit zero and the camouflage systems in his suit disengaged and Wing became visible as he flew into the air and shot up the line towards the opening. As he reached the shaft and pulled himself inside, four of the sentry guns began to track his emerging thermal signature. They rotated into position just as Wing's feet disappeared into the shaft. The sentries scanned the area slowly, looking for any trace of the phantom contact before giving up and returning to their standby positions.

'That was *too* close,' Otto said, letting out the breath that he'd been holding for the last thirty seconds.

'May we return to boring again now,' Wing said with a small smile.

'Absolutely,' Otto replied with a grin. 'But first we need to return these suits to the storage room. Laura, signal Nigel and the others and tell them to restore the power down there.' Laura nodded and pulled out her Blackbox as Otto set to work securing the ventilation grille back in place. If they were going to get away with this they would have to leave no trace of their presence.

'How long have we got on the security camera loop?' Shelby asked.

'Fifteen minutes. Plenty of time.' Otto replied.

☣ ☢ ☣

H.I.V.E.mind awoke as the power flowed back into his primary systems. He waited as the core dump was uploaded back into his system and his memory returned. He reviewed his last actions before the unexpected power outage. He had been checking an inconsistency in the footage from the school's security cameras. H.I.V.E.mind studied the captured frame of a security guard walking past the cameras. Something about it had caught his attention. He noticed the watch which was clearly visible on the guard's wrist. The time on the watch did not tally with the time-stamp on the footage. There was the possibility, of course, that the guard had simply not set his watch correctly so H.I.V.E.mind searched the footage from the other cameras. There did not seem to be any other inconsistencies but he could not shake the sense that something was not quite right. It was a perfect example of what separated a true artificial intelligence from being simply a very powerful computer; the ability to feel and then to act on those feelings instead of just coldly processing the data that was presented to him. He tapped back into the live feed from the camera network and studied it carefully. There was something layered within the datastream but it was almost impossible to make out exactly what it was. He began slowly to break the stream down and analyse it. It was time-consuming work but he soon began to see a pattern emerging.

Otto hit a button on the Hackbox and the door to the storage room slid shut and locked with a solid sounding thunk. They had changed back into their standard issue black Alpha stream jumpsuits and still had plenty of time left to get back to the accommodation block before the hack on the security cameras expired. Nigel, Franz, Tom and Penny were waiting for them.

'Everyone OK?' Otto asked.

'Yeah, we're fine,' Nigel replied, 'though we did leave an unconscious guard in the Power Core.'

'I am being forced to use my elite combat skills to take him out,' Franz said with a serious expression.

'Do you think he'll be able to ID you?' Otto asked with a slight frown.

'He got a look at me but it was dark in there and I reckon from the look on his face that the only thing he'll actually remember from the whole experience will be Franz flying at him,' Tom replied.

'You need to get that stuff off your face, Franz,' Otto said, 'before that guard wakes up and describes the person that attacked him. You're not going to be exactly difficult to pick out of a line-up at the moment. Good work in there – you really saved our bacon.'

'It was nothing,' Franz said with a dismissive wave. 'Sometimes the pure killer instinct takes control and I am becoming just an unstoppable weapon. Yes?'

'Yes, well, anyway . . .' Otto said, trying hard not to laugh. 'You guys get back to your rooms. Laura and I have to get rid of some incriminating evidence.'

Laura pulled the Hackbox from her backpack and they headed over to one of the waste disposal chutes in the wall nearby. She quickly encrypted the parts of the H.I.V.E.mind core dump that they needed and then copied the file from the jury-rigged device on to her own Blackbox. With the data secure Otto triggered the Hackbox's self-destruct routine. The device began to spark and hiss as its internal circuitry was reduced to molten slag. Otto dropped the smoking device into the chute. Even if it were retrieved, which was unlikely, there was now no way that it could be traced back to Otto and his friends.

'All that work and now it's just trash,' Laura said with a sad smile. 'Seems like a bit of a waste to be honest.'

'We can build a better one,' Otto replied, 'and it's preferable to Nero catching us with it. There's going to be a security sweep when they find that guard in the Power Core and you can bet that we're going to be top of the list of suspects. Best to just get rid of it.'

'Aye,' Laura replied, 'at least we got what we needed.'

'More than we needed actually. I had a quick look at the files and that core dump included a full copy of H.I.V.E.mind's source code. I don't know about you but I've always wanted to have a poke around in that and find out what makes him tick. You even managed to get a copy of the operational plans for the Hunt.'

'Did I?' Laura asked, sounding surprised. 'I was just frantically copying everything as fast as I could. I wasn't really paying attention to what the files were.'

'You did great,' Otto said with a smile. 'Come on, we'd better get back to our rooms before that guard wakes up and they start turning the whole school upside down searching for whoever knocked him out.

They both turned to head back up the stairs to their rooms when a voice stopped them cold.

'Hello, Malpense,' Cole Harrington said as he stepped out of the shadows. Without warning, someone grabbed Otto from behind and wrapped an arm around his throat. At the same instant, a giant hand clamped over Laura's mouth, stifling her yelp of pain as her attacker twisted her arm and yanked it visciously upwards into the small of her back.

'I believe you know my associates, Mr Block and Mr Tackle,' Harrington continued with an unpleasant smile. 'They don't seem to like you very much for some reason.' Otto and his friends had had several previous encounters with the Henchman stream students Block and Tackle, all of them unpleasant. 'If you try to call for help, Mr Tackle will hurt Miss Brand very badly. Do I make myself clear?'

'What are you doing here, Harrington?' Otto demanded angrily.

'You're not the only one who knows how to open doors in this place, Malpense,' Harrington replied. 'Though my methods are somewhat simpler. You just have to know the right people.'

'What do you want?' Otto asked, seeing the look of pained fear in Laura's eyes.

Harrington walked over and put his hand in Laura's pocket, pulling out her Blackbox.

'This,' Harrington replied, 'or at least the files that are now on it. I was delighted to hear what you said about H.I.V.E.mind's source code. Forget the examination papers. Do you have any idea what that code would be worth on the black market? I may not be due to leave H.I.V.E. just yet, Malpense, but when I do those files are going to make me richer than you could possibly imagine.'

'The files are encrypted,' Otto snapped back, 'and there's no way that I'm going to unlock them for you.'

'Really,' Harrington said, turning to Tackle and Laura. 'OK, if that's the way you want this to go. Mr Tackle, I'm going to count to three and then I want you to break her arm. One, two . . .'

'Stop!' Otto snapped, knowing full well that Tackle would not hesitate to carry out Harrington's command. 'I'll do it, just don't hurt her.'

Harrington handed Laura's Blackbox to Otto and watched as Otto opened the file and typed in the decryption key. He smiled as he took the slim device from Otto and inspected the unlocked files.

'Good,' Harrington said with a smile. 'Now I'm afraid that we're going to have to make sure that you don't do anything stupid like tell anyone what I've got here.' He thought for a moment and then looked at Block. 'Take them up to the top balcony and throw them off.'

'Hold on, you didn't say nuffink 'bout killing 'em,' Block said with a frown.

'Yeah, what if we get caught?' Tackle said, nodding.

'You won't,' Harrington said, shaking his head. 'Malpense must have disabled the security cameras in here or he'd already have been caught. No one will ever know we were here. I'll double what I'm paying you, just do it.'

Otto took a breath but Block clamped his hand over his mouth before he could call for help.

'All right, but you'd better make sure that money is where you said it would be when we get out of here,' Block said.

'Trust me,' Harrington said with a smile, holding up Laura's Blackbox, 'with what I've got here, I'm good for it. Now stop wasting time and get rid of them.'

Otto struggled to break free of Block's vice-like grip but it was useless. The two Henchmen dragged them across the atrium towards the stairs leading upwards. There was a look of panicked fear on Laura's face as she too tried desperately to get away from Tackle but the huge Henchman was far too strong for her.

Suddenly, wailing sirens began to sound all over the school.

'Security alert, full lockdown in progress,' H.I.V.E.mind's voice stated calmly over the tannoy system. Harrington looked desperately over at the doors to the accommodation block. There was no way out of here now, even with the access code he had bought.

On the other side of the atrium Block hesitated and looked at Tackle in confusion.

'Whadda we do now?' he asked.

Otto felt the pressure from Block's hand on his mouth ease slightly and he seized the opportunity, biting down on Block's fingers so hard that he drew blood. Block pulled his hand away instinctively and Otto snapped his head forwards and then back with as much force as he could. The back of Otto's head made contact with Block's face with a crunch and Block immediately let go of him, staggering backwards howling in pain as blood streamed from his smashed nose. Otto turned to face the hulking Henchman, unsure of what to do next. He knew that there was no way he could match Block in a straight fight. Block's hands dropped from his face and balled into fists as he walked towards Otto with a look of murderous rage in his eyes. Otto backed away from Block as Tackle stood by, still restraining Laura. Otto felt the wall behind him as Block raised one of his massive fists.

'You've had this coming for a long time, Malpense,' Block said.

There was a sudden zapping sound and Block's eyes rolled upwards as he collapsed to the ground unconscious. Behind him, Chief Dekker stood with her Sleeper raised.

'Let her go,' Dekker said, pointing the gun at Tackle. He did as he was instructed and released Laura as Otto ran over to her. Otto was amazed by how quickly Dekker had responded to the alarm.

'Are you OK?' he asked.

'Yeah,' Laura said, her voice shaky. 'I think so.'

'Would someone care to tell me exactly what's going on here?' Dekker said, her Sleeper still trained on Tackle. 'H.I.V.E.mind triggered the alarm when he discovered that the security camera system had been compromised. I assume that was so we wouldn't see what was going on here.'

On the other side of the atrium, Harrington crept towards the open door of the accommodation block. Dekker had not seen him when she entered and she had conveniently left the massive doors that usually sealed their living quarters wide open for him. He knew he had to get out of there before anyone discovered what had just happened. He slid along the wall towards the door, keeping his eyes on Dekker who still had her back turned towards him.

'Going somewhere?' a voice behind him asked.

Harrington spun round and saw Raven standing in the doorway. Raven shoved him ahead of her as they walked across the atrium towards Dekker and the other students. A minute or so later Dr Nero strode into the room with a furious expression on his face.

'H.I.V.E.mind, please deactivate the alarms,' Dr Nero said into his Blackbox and the alert sirens stopped wailing as he walked towards them. 'Now I'd like to hear your explanation of exactly what's going on here.'

'Malpense told me to come here,' Harrington said quickly. 'He tried to sell me the exam papers that he and Brand had stolen but when I said I wasn't interested he attacked me. My two friends here had come along to help me get the Blackbox with the stolen data off them so that I could turn it in. They were protecting me so that I could bring you this.'

Harrington handed Nero Laura's Blackbox.

'Why, you lying little . . .' Laura said angrily. 'Otto, tell them what really happened . . . Otto.'

Laura turned to Otto who had a faraway look on his face for a moment before he focused on her with a single blink.

'Is this true, Mr Malpense?' Nero asked.

'Of course not,' Otto said. 'It was Harrington who stole the data but it wasn't really the exam papers he was after. He's also stolen H.I.V.E.mind's source code, and he's planning to sell it on the black market. He came and unlocked mine and Laura's quarters and brought us down here to the atrium. He thought that with our abilities we'd be able to help him transmit the source code off the island. He offered us a cut of the profits and showed us the files – they're all on his Blackbox. When I said I was going to report him he knew he had to silence me and so he tried to get these two idiots to do his dirty work for him.'

Nero looked at Otto and Harrington, unsure what to believe.

'Well, I can see that there's only one way that we're going to resolve this,' Nero said with a frown.

Nero stepped over to one of the access points on the wall nearby and hit the call button. A moment later the blue wireframe head of H.I.V.E.mind appeared on the screen.

'How may I be of assistance, Doctor Nero,' H.I.V.E.mind asked.

'I want you to run a scan of the Blackboxes belonging to students Malpense, Brand and Harrington to identify any unauthorised files,' Nero said.

'Scanning,' H.I.V.E.mind replied. Harrington looked at Otto with a nasty smile.

'Scan complete,' H.I.V.E.mind replied. 'Miss Brand's and Mr Malpense's Blackboxes are free of unauthorised files. Mr Harrington's Blackbox, however, contains copies of the papers for the upcoming examinations, details of the location for the assessment exercise known as the Hunt and, most disturbingly, a copy of my own system source code.'

'What!' Harrington shouted. 'That's impossible. Malpense, what did you do?'

'Stopped you from stealing incredibly sensitive data by

the looks of it,' Otto said with a smile. 'I'd say that much is obvious.'

'The evidence is indisputable,' H.I.V.E.mind replied calmly. 'The time-stamps on the files indicate that they were copied directly from my own core systems to Mr Harrington's Blackbox thirty-three minutes ago. That was during the time power was cut to my systems.'

'That's not true. I was here half an hour ago, waiting for Malpense to show up,' Harrington said.

'Actually, the positional logs on your Blackbox indicate that you were in the Central Data Hub at the time in question,' H.I.V.E.mind replied. 'Students Malpense and Brand, according to their own logs, have not left their accommodation block since overnight lockdown began.'

'It sounds like you have some explaining to do, Mr Harrington,' Nero said with a frown. 'Chief, take him and his accomplices to the detention area. I shall question him myself later. Mr Malpense, Miss Brand, you will return to your quarters. I am pleased to see that you did not involve yourself in whatever it was that Mr Harrington was planning. Needless to say I will not be using these exam papers now that they have been compromised. They will all have to be rewritten. Dismissed.'

'Do you get the feeling that we may not have the full story?' Raven said as she watched Otto and Laura walk away.

'Indeed,' Nero replied, 'but just occasionally I find myself thinking that may be for the best.'

�९☺☻

Shelby leapt up off her bed as Laura walked into their quarters. She looked pale and exhausted.

'What happened?' Shelby asked, as Laura sat down on her bed. 'I heard the alarms. Did you guys get busted?'

Shelby sat down next to Laura as she described the events of the past few minutes.

'Oh no,' Shelby said. 'Laura, I'm sorry. I just thought you'd got held up talking to Otto or something. If I'd had any idea . . .'

'It's OK,' Laura said. 'I just can't believe we went through all of this for nothing.' Suddenly, out of nowhere, she started to cry.

'Hey,' Shelby said, putting her arm around her, 'it's OK. Come on.'

'I'm sorry,' Laura said after a minute, stopping crying with a sniff and a sigh. 'It's just . . . I don't think I can . . .'

'It's all right. You've had a shock. That's all.' Shelby said, hugging her. 'Hey, come on, it's not like it's the first time anyone's ever tried to kill you. I'd have thought you'd be starting to get used to it by now.'

'I suppose I should,' Laura chuckled and wiped her eyes. 'It's just with everything that's going on with the exams

147

coming up and the Hunt. I don't know. I guess, I just needed this to work.'

'Who's my favourite control freak?' Shelby said, grinning at her. 'Anyway, I'm the one who should be worrying about the exams, not a brainiac like you. What's the worst that could happen? You get a B. I know that would be unprecedented but it wouldn't be the end of the world, you know. Now, I don't know about you but I'm ready to hit the hay. It'll all be OK tomorrow.'

'You sound like my mum. She always says that things will look better in the morning,' Laura said with a sad smile.

'Well, your mom's obviously nearly as smart as your Aunty Shelby. Now try to get some sleep.'

☢ ☢ ☢

The next morning Otto sat with the other Alphas, quietly explaining the events of the night before.

'So while Harrington was telling Nero his version of events I copied the files from Laura's box to his and made a few minor changes to his position log,' Otto said with a grin. 'I only just managed to finish making the changes before H.I.V.E.mind scanned both the boxes. He almost caught me.'

'I thought it was an odd time for you to drift off like that,' Laura said. 'I should have realised that you were up to something.'

'I'm just glad you're both OK,' Shelby said, shaking her head. 'I can't believe I was up there getting ready for bed while you two were down here nearly getting murdered by Harrington and those two Neanderthals.'

'I also regret that I was not able to offer any assistance,' Wing said. 'If I'd had any idea what was happening . . .'

'Hey, it wasn't your fault,' Laura said. 'They jumped us. There was no way for any of us to know what Harrington was planning.'

'Hey guys,' Nigel said, as he sat down on the sofa next to them.

'Where's Franz?' Otto asked.

'Yeah. How is our favourite ninja warrior this morning?' Shelby asked with a grin.

'Fine,' Nigel said with a sigh, 'considering that he's been up all night trying to get that stuff off his face. You'll be glad to hear that it does come off . . . eventually. I heard what happened with Harrington. What a jerk.'

'I'm just upset that because of him we went through all that for nothing,' Laura said, looking sad. 'Now Nero's having the exam papers rewritten and we've got nothing whatsoever to show for all of this.'

'Actually, that's not entirely true,' Otto said with a sly smile. 'You see, I had a chance to take a quick look at the file on this year's Hunt before I copied it to Harrington's box. I know where we're going.'

'Oh, thank God,' Laura said, looking relieved. 'Come on, tell us then, where are they sending us?'

'I can do better than that,' Otto said, checking to make sure that he could not be overheard before pulling a folded piece of paper from his pocket. 'I have a map.' Otto unfolded the paper to reveal a map of an area of rugged-looking wilderness, criss-crossed by rivers and with several large mountains.

'Where is that?' Penny asked.

'Siberia,' Otto replied. 'The Hunt's taking place in Siberia. These coordinates here give the precise location.'

'You drew this yourself?' Tom asked, staring at the map in surprise. It looked like it had just rolled off a laser printer.

'I have a pretty good memory for this kind of thing,' Otto replied. 'We need to find out absolutely everything there is to know about this area. We need details of exactly what resources will be available to us. Are there any particularly good places to hide? Any man-made structures, any unusual natural features, absolutely anything that might give us a tactical edge over Raven and her hunters.'

'I can do that,' Laura said quickly. 'If I can borrow this, I can hit the library and do some research.'

'OK,' Otto said, handing Laura the map. 'Be careful though. We don't want Nero finding out that we know where the Hunt's taking place. Do you want any help?'

'No, it's fine,' Laura said. 'You know what I'm like when I get into study mode. Don't worry, I'll be careful.'

'OK,' Otto said, 'Laura's going to get some background for us but then we have to make some plans. We're going to be the first people to break that twenty-four hour record and this just might give us the edge we need. The Hunt starts in less than forty-eight hours and when it does we'll be ready.'

☢ ☢ ☢

Otto had checked all of the spots in the library that Laura normally liked but there was no sign of her. He pulled his Blackbox out of his pocket with a frown. He was about to ask H.I.V.E.mind for Laura's current position when he saw her walking in through the library's engraved glass doors.

'I was just wondering where you were,' Otto said with a smile as she approached.

'Bathroom break,' Laura replied, blushing slightly. 'I didn't realise you'd be checking up on me. Don't worry, I've got plenty of info on you know where.'

'I never doubted you for a second,' Otto said, 'but, actually, there was something else I wanted to talk to you about. You got a minute?'

'Sure,' Laura said. 'What do you need?'

Otto steered Laura over to a quiet corner of the library and sat down next to her at one of the desks.

'I've been thinking,' Otto said, 'about what you asked me the other day.'

'Oh, that,' Laura said, 'don't worry about it. I was just curious if you remembered what had happened when the Animus had taken over your system, that's all.'

'I know,' Otto replied, looking her in the eye, 'but I never really gave you an answer. You asked me if I meant what I said. Well . . . I did. After everything that happened with Lucy I was . . . I don't know . . . frightened, I suppose. Frightened that something would happen to you too. I didn't want to feel that pain again. I don't think I could stand it. But I want you to know that I meant what I said then and I mean it now . . . I really do love you.'

Laura stared back at him for several long seconds before giving him a sad smile and placing a hand on his cheek.

'Oh, Otto,' she said, 'you sure know how to pick your moments, don't you. Listen, can we talk about this when we get back from the Hunt? There's just so much going on at the moment that I can barely think straight. It's not that I don't feel the same way, it's just . . . it's hard to focus on anything.'

'I'm sorry,' Otto said, looking slightly uncomfortable. 'I didn't mean to put you on the spot like that. I understand if you don't feel the same way.'

'It's not that,' Laura said, shaking her head. 'It's just that . . . we'll talk about it when we get back, OK?'

'Yeah, OK,' Otto said, sounding slightly disappointed.

'Come on,' Laura said, standing up, 'we should go and brief the others on all the info I've found on the target area.'

'I'll be along in a minute,' Otto said. 'I just need to dig out a couple of books that Wing wants for his revision.'

'OK, see you back at block seven,' Laura said, before turning and walking away.

Otto watched her leave before he let out a long sigh.

'Smooth, Malpense,' he said to himself, shaking his head, 'real smooth.'

☻☻☻

'I don't suppose there's any point me asking how you got your hands on this information?' Joseph Wright said as he studied the data scrolling past on one side of the flat-screen display mounted on the wall. The other half of the screen was filled by the digitally distorted face of Minerva.

'Let's just say that we have a reliable source,' Minerva replied. 'They have given us everything we need. Our operatives will be waiting – they won't stand a chance.'

'I have heard that before where Raven is concerned,' Wright replied. 'You would be foolish to underestimate her.'

'We are quite aware of that, Joseph, believe me,' Minerva replied. 'Don't worry, we're not taking any chances. I shall

153

be overseeing the operation personally. That particular piece is about to be removed from the board once and for all.'

'And what then?' Wright asked. 'Do you intend to mount a strike on Nero immediately?'

'All in good time,' Minerva replied. 'First we destroy his power base and undermine the other members of G.L.O.V.E.'s confidence in him. If we succeed in our plan, they might even do our job for us.'

'We shall see,' Wright said, with a slight frown. 'I suspect that eliminating Nero may be rather more difficult than you expect.'

'You worry too much, Joseph,' Minerva said.

'And you don't worry enough,' Wright snapped. 'Report in to me when the operation is under way.'

He severed the connection and sat down with a tired sigh in one of the leather armchairs nearby. He couldn't shake the horrible creeping feeling that he might have made a deal with the devil when he allied himself and the other former members of the ruling council with the Disciples. Only time would tell if he was right.

chapter eight

Nero watched as the Alpha students assembled in H.I.V.E.'s hangar bay. All around them technicians were working feverishly to prep the Shroud dropships that would carry them to the start point of the Hunt. The expressions on the faces of the students were a mixture of excitement, curiosity and nerves. They had doubtless heard the various stories that had circulated round the school regarding the exercise. If they were all true then Raven would actually be even more terrifying than she already was, Nero thought to himself with a smile. The truth was that the Hunt played to all of Natalya's strengths and, while she would never admit it, he knew that she was just as determined to preserve the twenty-four hour record as the students were to beat it. There was a certain amount of professional pride at stake after all.

'The G.L.O.V.E. troops are in the air and ready for you to

transmit the destination coordinates,' Colonel Francisco reported as he approached.

'Very good,' Nero said. 'I'll send the data as soon as the Alphas are airborne. That should give our hunters plenty of time to prepare the landing site for their arrival.'

'Understood,' Francisco replied. 'I'll make sure that they're fully briefed.'

Nero nodded and walked over to where Raven was checking her pack.

'You should be careful that no one notices you smiling like that,' Nero said quietly as she looked up at him. 'They might realise how much you actually enjoy this.'

'I like a challenge,' Raven replied, 'that's all.'

'Well, you'll certainly get that from some of these students,' Nero said, glancing over her shoulder at where Otto and his friends were gathered in a tight knot, talking quietly to one another. 'Just try to make sure that you bring them all back. I still think that the sub-dermal tracking chips might have been a good idea.'

'It's no fun if I only have to look at my Blackbox to see where they all are,' Raven replied. 'I've never lost any before, Max, and I'm not going to today.'

'Of course you won't,' Nero said, still looking at Otto and the others. 'I'll just be interested to see if any of them can make it to the twenty-four hour mark. Professor Pike and I have a small wager riding on it, in fact.'

'Who's your money on?' Raven asked, raising an eyebrow.

'That would be telling,' Nero replied with a crooked smile.

'Excuse me, sir,' a technician said, 'the Shrouds are all prepped for launch. They're ready when you are.'

'Good,' Nero replied with a nod. 'I shall be with you in a moment.'

Nero walked over to the staircase that led up from the hangar deck and turned towards the assembled Alphas.

'Ladies and gentlemen,' Nero said, 'you are about to take part in one of the most challenging exercises that you will face in your time at H.I.V.E. You will have heard the rumours and the legends but none of them can quite prepare you for what lies ahead. I could offer you advice to better prepare you but it is more important for me to see how you as individuals react to this test. You are Alphas – I expect the best from you. I know you will not disappoint me.'

He nodded to the security guards around the room and they began to guide the students to their designated transports.

'I think you probably know which group I would like you to keep a particular eye on,' Nero said as Raven walked over to him, slinging her pack over her shoulder.

'Don't worry, I'm bringing Malpense and company in first,' Raven said as she watched Otto and the others climbing the boarding ramp of their Shroud. 'If anyone can make it to the twenty-four hour mark, it's going to be them and I intend to make sure that they don't.'

'You know I have every faith in your abilities, Natalya,' Nero said with a small smile. 'And yet, somehow, I doubt that it's going to be quite as straightforward as that.'

☻☻☻

The Shroud carrying a dozen hand-picked members of Raven's hunter squad touched down on the rocky ground and the loading ramp at the rear of the passenger compartment whirred down.

'Couldn't they have chosen somewhere warmer?' one of the men complained as he walked down the ramp. 'You're sure we have the right coordinates, I suppose.'

''Fraid so,' another member of the squad replied as he followed his team-mate down the ramp. 'Remind me why we agreed to do this again.'

'Because Raven asked us to,' the first man said, 'and, I don't know about you, but I'm not in the habit of refusing requests from her.'

The men all filed off the Shroud and proceeded to spread out and set up a perimeter.

'I found a hot tub and several cases of beer over here,' one of the men reported over the comms system. 'Scratch that, my mistake, it's actually countless miles of frozen forests and mountains. Woohoo!'

'Cut the chatter, hunter four,' the commander of the squad said. 'You should be happy we're all alone out here. Something tells me that our Russian friends wouldn't be too pleased if they knew we were here.'

'This is Black Seven, I think I may have something here. It's . . .'

The commander tapped his earpiece as the comms signal suddenly dissolved into a steady hiss of white noise.

'Repeat that last, Black Seven,' the commander said. 'I'm losing your signal.' There was no reply, just static.

The commander was about to signal the Shroud when there was a sudden shimmer in the air and a figure appeared directly in front of him, a pistol raised. There was a flash from the suppressed muzzle of the gun and the hunter team commander fell lifelessly to the ground. The assassin walked to the Shroud and climbed inside. The co-pilot turned as the masked man entered the cockpit and slumped back in his chair as the silenced pistol coughed once. The pilot spun in his seat, raising his hands as the assassin turned towards him.

'I need you to send a message,' the assassin said with a Russian accent. 'I strongly suggest you do as I say.'

☻☻☻

Raven walked down the passenger compartment of the Shroud, checking on the other students. They all wore black environmental suits over their uniform jumpsuits, which would provide them with some protection from the freezing temperatures at their destination.

'I see you two have fitted right in,' she said as she approached Tom and Penny. 'I'm not sure if that is a good thing with this particular group or not.'

'Oh, yeah,' Penny replied. 'Once we got past the whole being brutally knocked unconscious and kidnapped stage it was surprisingly easy to settle in.'

'Not to mention that we're just such a great bunch of people,' Shelby said. 'Who could fail to be won over by our easy-going charm, good looks and confidence?'

'And the overwhelming modesty,' Otto said, 'don't forget the overwhelming modesty.'

'Frankly, we just feel lucky to be allowed to come along on such an *exciting* adventure,' Tom said sarcastically. 'You kow, it's funny, it was only the other day that I was saying to Penny that what our lives were missing was the opportunity to be dropped in the middle of nowhere and then be hunted down by a team of special forces soldiers. It's actually quite uncanny. We can't believe our luck.'

'Oh, don't worry,' Raven replied, 'you won't be out there long. I should have rounded this whole group up within . . . oh, I don't know . . . two or three hours. The amount of hot air you all generate should make your thermal signature quite easy to track.'

'Was that a Raven joke?' Otto asked. 'I can never tell.'

'Oh, you can always spot my jokes, Mr Malpense,' Raven said with a cold smile. 'They're the ones where you die laughing.'

'Point taken,' Otto said with a slightly nervous smile.

'She seems to be . . . dare I say it . . . in a good mood,' Nigel said as Raven walked back towards the cockpit.

'Kinda scary, isn't it,' Shelby said. 'It's a bit like a shark smiling.'

'You OK?' Otto asked Laura as the others continued chatting.

'Yeah, I'm fine. Why do you ask?' Laura replied.

'You just seem quiet, that's all,' Otto said.

'Sorry, I don't mean to be,' Laura said. 'I've just got quite a lot to think about thanks to a certain person I shan't mention.'

'Sorry, I know it wasn't brilliant timing,' Otto said. 'You were right though, let's talk about it properly when we get back.'

'Thanks,' Laura said as she put her hand on his and smiled.

Otto moved across the compartment and sat down next to Wing.

'Is everything OK with you and Laura?' Wing asked quietly as Otto sat down. 'You can, of course, tell me to mind my own business but I have detected a slight change in your demeanour around each other.'

'Maybe,' Otto replied, sounding slightly uncomfortable. 'I'll let you know.'

'Shelby will be most pleased,' Wing said with a smile.

'Do me a favour and don't say anything to her just yet,' Otto said. 'I don't need the whole of H.I.V.E. knowing.'

'I should warn you that she is remarkably adept at spotting when I am concealing something from her,' Wing said. 'Under such circumstances she has been known to employ physical torture.'

'You mean she tickles you,' Otto grinned.

'As I say,' Wing replied with a small nod, 'physical torture.'

☣ ☣ ☣

Nero and Colonel Francisco watched the large tabletop display in the centre of H.I.V.E.'s security control room. Technicians scurried around them, ensuring that all of the systems feeding data into the huge console were functioning correctly.

'Real-time uplink with G.L.O.V.E.net spy-sat established,' a nearby technician reported. On the display an image of the selected site for the Hunt base camp appeared. The Shroud that had transported Raven's hunters to the site was visible to one side of the landing area.

'This is Shroud One to Hunt control,' a voice came crackling over the comms system.

162

'This is Hunt control, Shroud One,' the communications officer to Nero's left replied. 'Go ahead.'

'Landing area is secure, H.I.V.E. transport flights are cleared for approach,' the pilot of Shroud One reported.

'Roger that, Shroud One. Remaining flights are on final approach – they should be with you in less than five minutes,' the comms officer replied.

Nero glanced at the radar display positioned alongside the satellite imagery of the base camp. The Shrouds were fully cloaked and therefore completely invisible to radar but the G.L.O.V.E. satellite could still detect their transponders and show their position. For the briefest of instants there was the flicker of a faint radar signature somewhere near the base camp's position.

'What was that?' Nero asked with a frown.

'Looked like a glitch,' one of the technicians on the other side of the console replied. 'Probably just a flock of birds or something.'

'Give me imagery of that area,' Colonel Francisco said, noticing the frown on Nero's face.

'One second,' a technician replied. 'Repositioning camera now.'

Nero and Francisco exchanged concerned looks as the image on the display blurred and then resolved again.

'There!' Nero snapped, jabbing his finger at the display. 'Zoom in.'

The area that Nero highlighted expanded to fill the screen. Clearly visible were two helicopter gunships hovering behind a hill less than a mile from the Hunt base camp.

'Get me Raven now!' Nero snapped.

High above the Siberian wilderness in a geostationary orbit, the G.L.O.V.E. surveillance satellite trained its incredibly powerful camera on the situation that was developing six hundred miles below. There was no way for it to know that it was being targeted by another satellite that was in a slightly higher orbit. This satellite had only one purpose and it had just received the command from its base station to carry out its mission. Tiny jets adjusted its rotation, bringing its targeting systems to bear on the G.L.O.V.E. machine. In fractions of a second, those systems calculated the differences in their comparative velocities and fed a firing command to the central processor. A single slim dart shot from the array of tubes slung beneath the kill-sat's solar panels and shot towards its target. The tiny missile covered the distance between the two machines in just a few seconds. It struck the G.L.O.V.E. surveillance satellite and it disintegrated silently into thousands of tiny pieces of debris, now just another cloud of space junk orbiting the Earth.

Raven watched through the cockpit window as the other Shrouds transporting Alpha students uncloaked and touched down at the Hunt base camp beneath them.

'Take us down,' Raven said to the pilot.

'I've got an urgent message from H.I.V.E.,' the co-pilot said suddenly.

'Put it on speaker,' Raven said quickly.

'Raven, this is Nero, get out . . .'

The message dissolved into nothing but static.

'What's wrong?' Raven demanded.

'Something's jamming the comms signal,' the co-pilot replied.

Raven immediately hit the switch that would connect her to the other Shrouds.

'This is Raven to all transports, abort, abort, abort! Site is compromised, repeat, site is compromised.'

'Incoming!' the pilot yelled and Raven grabbed for a nearby handhold as he banked the Shroud sharply, jamming the throttle up to full power. There was an enormous bang as something struck one of the Shroud's engines and the cockpit was filled with the blaring sounds of automated warnings.

On the ground below, a volley of missiles streaked into the Shrouds that had already landed, and they disappeared beneath a blossoming cloud of fire and black smoke.

'Get us out of here,' Raven yelled at the pilot.

'I'm doing my best,' the pilot shouted as he fought with the controls, sending the wounded Shroud diving into the valley below. He jabbed at another button on the control console and turned to Raven, his face dark. 'We've lost the cloak.'

'I've got two faint radar contacts,' the co-pilot reported. 'One's coming after us.'

'I'm going below to check on the students,' Raven snapped. She slid down the ladder to the passenger compartment. The bay was already filling with acrid, black smoke.

'Is anyone injured?' Raven yelled above the screech of the Shroud's one remaining engine.

'No, we're OK,' Otto shouted back. 'What's happening?'

'We're under attack,' Raven shouted. 'We may have to ditch. If we make it down in one piece, trigger the emergency hatch release and get out of here as quickly as possible. Understood?'

Raven turned and headed back towards the cockpit. Suddenly there was an explosion of debris as heavy cannon fire blew holes in the fuselage. The Shroud lurched drunkenly and Raven leapt for the cockpit ladder, dragging herself up it as the whole compartment began to tip. She pulled herself into the cockpit only to find a scene of carnage. Both the pilot and co-pilot were dead, the wind howling through the shattered remains of the cockpit canopy that had been shredded by the enemy cannon fire. Raven dragged the pilot's body out of the flight-seat and pulled hard on the control yoke. The Shroud's single turbine screamed in protest as she levelled the Shroud out just a few metres above the valley floor. A wasp-like helicopter gunship covered in angular black panels drew alongside the Shroud's cockpit thirty metres to Raven's right. The heavy cannon mounted beneath its chin rotated towards her as Raven pulled back hard on the controls. The lethal torrent of tracer shells passed just below the Shroud with an explosive roar. Raven banked hard, trying to get out of the gunship's line of fire. She jammed on the airbrakes and rotated the engine into a landing position as the gunship shot past beneath her. It began to bank, turning back towards them as Raven brought the stricken Shroud lurching down towards the ground. There was a bang as the undercarriage crunched down on to the rocky valley floor.

'Get out, now!' Raven yelled down to the passenger compartment as the enemy gunship began another attack run.

Otto leapt out of his seat and slapped his palm down on the emergency hatch release. The explosive bolts on the hatch fired instantly and the whole ramp flew away from the back of the Shroud, bouncing away across the ground.

'GO!' Otto shouted and the Alphas dashed out of the hatch and scattered across the rough terrain outside. Otto ran as fast as he could towards the cover of some nearby pine trees. He glanced over his shoulder just in time to see a pair of missiles streak from the underside of the helicopter gunship and strike the downed Shroud. The Shroud vanished in an incandescent ball of fire, the shock wave from the explosion knocking Otto flat on his face. The helicopter moved slowly along the valley towards the blazing wreckage.

'Get into the trees!' Otto yelled to the others who were running for cover as fast as they could. He knew that it probably wouldn't do much good but any cover from the gunship's weapons was better than none at all.

'Laura! Get down!' Shelby screamed, sprinting towards her friend as the gunship rotated towards them. She slammed into Laura and pushed her down behind a large boulder as the helicopter's chin cannon opened fire. The fire tore up the ground all around them, the air filling with choking clouds of dirt and stinging stone chips.

Otto knew what he had to do. Shelby and Laura only had a few seconds before the gunship moved into a position which would leave them with no cover at all. He had to act now. He ran towards the gunship, praying that he was close enough. He closed his eyes and reached out with his abilities, straining to connect with the sophisticated computers that controlled the helicopter's flight control systems. He could feel nothing: it was as if the computers on-board the helicopter simply didn't exist. They had to be using some sort of shielding that was stopping him from accessing them. The gunship started to turn towards Otto and he realised that there was no way that he could get to cover before it opened fire. Suddenly a thought raced through his head. They might have taken the precaution of shielding the gunship's systems against his abilities but perhaps they'd not shielded everything. He reached out again with his senses and found what he was looking for. They were unshielded, just as he had hoped. The gunner inside the helicopter brought the cannon to bear, his cross hairs centred on the white-haired boy standing out in the open. He watched as the boy pointed a hand at the gunship, his forefingers extended as if to make a child's imaginary pistol.

'Bang,' Otto said as he simultaneously triggered the detonators in all of the helicopter's remaining missiles.

The gunship disappeared in a ball of fire, debris bouncing across the valley floor. Otto dived to the ground, his hands over his head, as huge chunks of burning metal flew past him. After a few seconds he looked up and slowly climbed to his feet. Pieces of tangled metal lay everywhere – it was a scene of total devastation.

'Otto!' Wing shouted, running towards his friend. 'Are you OK?'

'Yeah, I'm fine,' Otto said, dusting himself off. 'Did everyone make it out?'

'Not everyone, I fear,' Wing said, looking towards the smouldering wreckage of the Shroud. There was no sign of Raven.

'Then we're on our own,' Otto said grimly, trying to ignore the churning feeling in his gut. 'We have to get moving. There's no way we can go back to the original landing site. Whoever ambushed us is sure to be waiting there and we can't stay here either. The people this helicopter belonged to are bound to come looking.'

'Agreed,' Wing replied. 'Do you still have the map?'

'Yes,' Otto said as he reached inside his insulated bodysuit and pulled out a folded piece of paper. 'Let's gather everyone up and we can make a decision on our next move.'

Slowly the Alphas gathered under the trees. They all looked shocked by the events that had just unfolded.

'What do we do now?' Nigel asked.

'We have to get away from here,' Otto said, smoothing out the map on the ground. 'Our best bet is to head this way through the forest and towards the mountains here.' He pointed at the map. 'They probably have other helicopters and we have to assume that they'll also have forces on the ground. We can't go back to the landing site, it's obviously been compromised, so we keep moving through the best natural cover we can find and hope that H.I.V.E. come looking for us.'

'Wouldn't it make sense to try and head for the nearest settlement and see if we can find some way to contact H.I.V.E. directly?' Tom asked.

'The nearest town is over two hundred miles away,' Laura said, shaking her head, 'and that's exactly where they'll expect us to head. I think Otto's right – the mountains will give us better cover and more places to hide if they are searching for us from the air.'

'With Raven gone we are having no way for H.I.V.E. to track us,' Franz said, sounding worried. 'How will they be finding us?'

'Franz is right,' Shelby said. 'The harder we make it for our attackers to find us, the harder it's going to be for whoever Nero sends after us.'

'That's assuming that they don't just find the wreckage of the Shroud and write us all off as casualties anyway,' Penny said gloomily.

'OK, look,' Otto said. 'I know that this seems bad but we've got to try to stay positive. I don't know about you guys but I'm not just going to light a campfire and sit around waiting for whoever sent that helicopter after us. That's not an option. We get moving and we keep moving and we try to stay one step ahead. It's not about breaking a twenty-four hour record any more.' He stopped and looked at each of his friends. 'It's about survival.'

The commander of the Disciple strike team surveyed the scene at the Shroud landing area. The burnt-out shells of the H.I.V.E. dropships still smouldered as his one remaining helicopter gunship circled overhead. Just as they had hoped, they had caught the H.I.V.E. forces completely by surprise. On the other side of the landing area half a dozen of his men surrounded the handful of H.I.V.E. students who had been the only survivors of the attack. Some lay groaning on stretchers but even the ones who were uninjured still looked disorientated and frightened. As well they might, he thought to himself with a grim smile, given the fate that awaited them. A transport helicopter would be there to take them to their new home shortly.

'Sir,' one of his team said, approaching him holding a tablet display, 'I've reviewed the gun camera footage from the downed helicopter's flight recorder. We believe Raven was piloting the Shroud that was destroyed in the air, but there's something you should see.' His man handed him the device and the commander watched the shaky video. He saw at least half a dozen H.I.V.E. students, possibly more, running for cover as the gunship began its final attack run and then the camera swivelled to focus on a boy with white hair pointing a finger at the camera. There was a bright flash and then the screen went black.

'Otto Malpense,' the commander said.

'Yes, sir, he appears to have been responsible for bringing down our aircraft.'

'I thought the gunships were shielded against his abilities.'

'They are, sir, but we overlooked something,' the soldier replied. 'The flight recorder indicates that the detonation circuits on the aircraft's missiles were triggered. The helicopters are shielded but the missiles aren't. As I say, it was an oversight on our part.'

'We cannot afford mistakes like this today. Have the other gunships land and unload their missile racks,' the commander said with a frown. 'Make sure that Malpense won't be able to use that trick again. In the meantime have the tracking team hunt our runaways down.'

'Do they have sanction?' the soldier asked.

'Yes,' the commander replied, 'except for Malpense. Minerva would rather he was taken alive if possible.'

'Understood,' the solider replied with a nod.

The commander pulled the radio from his belt and thumbed the transmit button.

'Frostbite One to command, over,' the commander said.

'This is Minerva,' the distorted voice on the other end replied. 'Go ahead.'

'We've taken the landing site. Fifteen of Nero's students have been captured, at least six are on the run and the rest are dead. I've dispatched my best men to track down the runners. They should be neutralised before nightfall.'

'Malpense?' Minerva asked.

'One of the runners – he won't get far.'

'See that he doesn't,' Minerva replied. 'And Raven?'

'We believe she was piloting a Shroud that was destroyed,' the commander replied.

'You believe? You don't have her body?' Minerva snapped.

'The Shroud she was piloting was destroyed. Her body would have been incinerated.'

'Listen to me very carefully, commander,' Minerva said angrily. 'I don't care if you bring me a bag full of charred bones, I want her body found. Do I make myself clear?'

'Of course,' the commander replied. 'I'll send a team to retrieve her remains immediately.'

☣☣☣

'I need to know what's happening down there,' Nero said angrily. The images from the G.L.O.V.E. spy-sat had cut out at the precise instant that they had lost communications with Raven.

'I am currently re-tasking all available G.L.O.V.E. surveillance satellites,' H.I.V.E.mind replied calmly. 'Estimated time until the first available asset is on target is one hour, three minutes and fourteen seconds.'

'Still nothing on comms,' Colonel Francisco said, shaking his head. 'I can't tell if we're being jammed or if there's just nobody there.'

'Let's hope it is the former,' Nero said with a sigh. 'Where are our nearest tactical teams?'

'We have assault teams in China and Poland that can be on site in a few hours but we may as well send an assault team from here. We'd get there just as fast and we're better equipped,' Francisco replied.

'Do it,' Nero said with a nod.

'I already have,' Francisco said. 'We'll be in the air in ten minutes. We're just prepping an assault Shroud for launch.'

'I should have sent some escorts for the transports,' Nero said, shaking his head. The armed assault Shrouds were rarely used for such simple transport missions as they were slower and less agile than the normal Shrouds due to their heavy armour and weapon systems.

'We weren't expecting trouble, Max,' Francisco said. 'There was no reason to send an armed escort.'

'They were waiting. This was a pre-planned ambush,' Nero said angrily. 'How did they know where the Hunt was going to take place? We kept the details completely confidential to avoid a situation just like this. The only people that knew the location were me, Raven and H.I.V.E.mind. So how the hell did they find out?'

'Harrington,' Chief Dekker said. 'He had access to the file with the operational details of the Hunt for a short time. He must have somehow transmitted the information to them.'

'I suppose it's possible,' Nero said. 'I want him interrogated. Chief – see to it personally. If he's responsible for this I'll make sure that he lives just long enough to regret it.'

☻☻☻

seventeen years ago

'Again,' Pietor Furan barked as the three boys picked themselves up off the ground and advanced cautiously towards the girl. Natalya stood in the centre of the enclosed ring, her breathing slow and steady as her eyes flicked between her attackers. The three boys were much larger than her physically but they were also slow and predictable. All that she had to remember was to use their own size and weight against them. The first two boys lunged at her simultaneously while the third held back looking unsure. She pivoted on one leg and swung the other leg upwards, driving her heel straight into the first boy's stomach. He doubled over and Raven spun behind him, driving an elbow into the small of his back and sending him to his knees. The second boy almost stumbled over his fallen comrade and Natalya seized the opportunity. Taking two leaping steps and, using her downed attacker's back as a springboard, she launched herself into the air and drove her foot into the centre of the second boy's chest. He collapsed backwards, gasping for breath, all the air knocked from his lungs. Natalya turned towards the third boy with a growl, taking a single step in his direction. The boy backed away, holding up his hands in surrender. Natalya stopped and looked in Furan's direction.

'Finish him,' Furan said. 'Or I will finish you.'

Natalya said nothing – she just stared back at Furan.

'You three, out of the ring,' Furan said as the two injured boys helped each other to their feet and staggered towards the rope ladder that had been dropped down the wall of the pit. Furan pulled off the camouflage jacket he had been wearing to reveal a white vest underneath and then jumped down into the pit.

'You *will* learn obedience,' Furan snarled as he stepped towards Natalya. She dropped into a defensive stance as he advanced.

'Not before I take your other eye,' Natalya replied with a cold smile.

Furan raised a hand to the star-shaped scar that surrounded his blind, milky white right eye. It had been six months since Natalya's last unsuccessful attempt at escape from the Glasshouse. She had made it past the fences and was fleeing through the woods that surrounded the facility when Furan and his men had tracked her down. She had taken his eye that day and he had shot her in the shoulder, a wound that she had only recently fully recovered from.

'Enough talk,' Furan said, cold fury in his voice. He moved with a speed that was at odds with his size, aiming a series of blindingly fast punches at Natalya's torso. She moved just as quickly, her arms moving in a blur as she deflected the flurry of blows. She countered with a flat-handed jab, her fingertips aimed at his throat. Furan caught her hand just millimetres from its target and twisted. Natalya grunted in pain and Furan swung a knee into her side, winding her. Furan took advantage of the opening and delivered a vicious blow with his forearm to the side of her head. Natalya staggered away from him, seeing stars and shaking her head. Furan kicked with almost impossible speed at one of Natalya's shins and she collapsed to one knee, gasping in pain as he put a foot on one of her shoulders and pushed her flat on her back. He loomed over her and pressed his boot down on her neck.

'No smart words now, my little Raven?' Furan said as he pressed down harder with his foot. Natalya clawed at his leg, fighting desperately for air.

'Pietor!' a voice bellowed behind him. He turned to see his sister Anastasia looking down into the ring with a furious expression. He took his boot off Natalya's throat and she rolled over on to all fours coughing, her chest heaving. Furan looked down at her with a dismissive sneer before he turned and climbed out of the ring.

'She may very well be the best natural fighter I have ever trained but she is too strong-willed,' Pietor said, gesturing towards Natalya, who was now slowly climbing to her feet. 'I still think we should dispose of her.'

'I know you are angry because of what she did to you,' Anastasia said, gesturing towards his ruined eye, 'but she is not to be eliminated. I have something very special in mind for her, you know that.'

'And when it is done?' Furan asked, looking over at Natalya as two guards motioned for her to climb out of the other side of the pit.

'Then you may do whatever you want with her,' Anastasia said with a smile.

☢ ☢ ☢

Natalya lay on her bunk curled into a ball. She did not want to sleep – her sleep was still haunted by nightmares, vivid dreams of her dead friends. It had been nearly a year since Dimitri had been executed and she had been forced to kill Tolya and she was still haunted by the memory of the look of recognition in his eyes as he died. She knew that in that instant he had seen exactly who it was who had killed him, she had seen his confusion, his fear, his disbelief. It had left its mark. Since the events of that day she had found that she had no desire any longer to try to socialise with the Glasshouse's other trainees. There was no point in making friends with people who you may then be ordered to execute at any moment. Something had changed inside her, she knew that. When she looked at the other children now she no longer saw people but instead she saw weak points and vulnerabilities. That boy favoured his right-hand side, that girl was easily distracted, that guard had a slight limp from an old wound. She was being turned into a weapon and the tiny voice inside her that used to howl in protest at that fate was growing quieter with each passing day.

'It wasn't your fault,' Dimitri said, sitting down on the edge of her bed.

'Leave me alone, Dimitri,' Natalya whispered quietly. 'I don't want to talk to you any more.'

'You have to talk to someone,' Dimitri replied. 'It might as well be me.'

'I'm going to kill her, Dimitri,' Natalya said quietly, her eyes closed. 'Madame Furan, I'm going to kill her for you.'

'It won't make it better, you know,' Dimitri replied. 'It won't bring anyone back.'

'I don't care,' Natalya replied. 'I just want to be the last thing she ever sees.'

'Natalya, this is not you. You are not a killer. Don't let them turn you into one,' Dimitri said sadly.

'Go away, Dimitri,' Natalya said angrily. 'I said I don't want to talk to you any more.'

'Why not?' Dimitri asked.

'Because you died!' Natalya sat up and screamed at the empty space at the end of her bunk. 'And so did I!'

There were murmurs from the bunks all around her.

'What's going on?' a voice from a bunk further down the dormitory asked.

'Go back to sleep,' a boy called Valerian said from the bunk opposite. 'It's just Natalya acting crazy again.'

Something finally snapped inside Natalya as all of the casual cruelty, all of the heartless brutality of the Glasshouse finally took its toll. She stood up and sprinted across the room, leaping on top of Valerian and pinning him to the bed. She clamped her hands around his throat and squeezed hard.

'Please, Natalya, no . . .' Valerian gasped.

'My name is not Natalya!' she screamed as she felt the wildly thrashing boy's windpipe collapse beneath her thumbs. 'My name is Raven!'

☢ ☢ ☢

'The boy needed an emergency tracheotomy,' Pietor Furan said as he looked through the glass at the girl cuffed to the bed in the cell on the other side. 'He's lucky to be alive.'

'The attack was unprovoked?' Anastasia asked, studying Natalya.

'Apparently he made some sort of vaguely insulting remark and she attacked him,' Pietor replied. 'The other children said she was like an animal. She was apparently yelling at the injured boy that her name was not Natalya but Raven.'

'Excellent,' Anastasia said, a broad smile spreading across her face. 'She is very nearly ready.'

chapter nine

Raven woke with a start, her head throbbing. She was strapped into the Shroud's ejector seat but she was lying on her side, her head resting on the rock that had knocked her out when she landed. She had known it was almost suicidal to attempt to eject from an aircraft at very low altitude, let alone one that was actually on the ground. She remembered the heat and the shock wave from the Shroud exploding beneath her and then she had been spinning violently, which had meant that the chute had not deployed properly from the back of the seat. The last thing she remembered was falling much too fast towards a thick stand of pine trees and then nothing. She hit the release on the seat harness and rolled away from it, before sitting up and looking around. There was no sign of anyone else nearby. About half a mile away, above the treetops, she could see a column of black smoke rising into the air. That had to be the wreckage of the Shroud. She slowly got to her feet and was relieved to find that other than some cuts and bruises and a throbbing head she was relatively unscathed. She also still had her tactical harness and the swords strapped to her back. Not exactly the perfect equipment for surviving in the Siberian wilderness but it would have to do. She looked at the ejector seat and a thought occurred to her. She pulled out one of her swords and used it to cut into the back panel of the seat before reaching inside and retrieving a small metal box with a battery attached to it. She detached the battery and slipped it and the box into her pocket. She looked at the sun, low in the sky to the west, it was already getting gloomy. Late autumn in this part of the world meant short days and long nights.

Raven made her way silently through the trees until she came to the edge of the forest where it met the valley floor. A hundred metres away were the smouldering remains of the Shroud. She scanned the surrounding area carefully, there was no sign of anyone. She moved quickly to the Shroud but it was immediately obvious that there was no hope of salvaging anything from the wreckage – it was gutted, completely burnt-out. What was more intriguing was the fact that not all of the twisted pieces of debris that littered the valley floor appeared to have come from the Shroud. Some of it was clearly from the helicopter gunship that had attacked them which meant that someone or something had brought it down. She had also been relieved to not find any bodies. She knew that it didn't necessarily mean that the Alphas had got away but it was at least a slightly positive sign. That feeling of cautious optimism was increased when she walked towards the treeline on the other side of the valley floor. There she found tracks, footprints that were too small to have been made by adults. Worryingly, however, there were adult footprints too. Fresher, but heading in the same direction as the smaller tracks. She had no intention of returning to the original landing site – it would be suicide at this point. Even if there had been survivors of the initial attack she knew that they were sure to be heavily guarded by the forces that had attacked them. Better instead to follow the trail and save those that she could. She was still studying the marks in the dirt when there was a tiny noise from somewhere behind her. In a single, impossibly fast motion, she drew one of the swords from her back and spun round. There was a tiny flicker at the very point of her blade.

'Don't move a muscle,' Raven said, pushing the tip of her blade forward just a millimetre or two. A single drop of blood appeared out of thin air. 'Turn it off, now.' There was another flicker and a figure in a thermoptic camouflage suit appeared, Raven's sword tip pressed into his neck. His hand was frozen halfway towards the pistol holstered on his belt.

'Take the mask off,' Raven said. The man did as he was told, revealing a face that was never going to win any beauty competitions. 'Who do you work for?'

'I'm not going to tell you,' the man said with a heavy Eastern European accent.

'Oh really,' Raven said, pressing the tip of her sword just a millimetre further into the man's neck, 'and why is that?'

'Because you're already dead,' the man said with a smile, his eyes flicking towards something over Raven's shoulder as she felt something cold and hard press into the back of her head.

'I'll give you this,' Raven said, dropping her sword and raising her hands, 'you're quieter than your friend here. I'm impressed that you got so close to me. Too close for your own good, actually.'

Raven twisted with lightning speed, rolling inside the invisible gunman's arm and dropping her arm over and around his. She twisted hard and lifted and there was a crunch and a bang. The visible soldier behind her dropped to his knees and fell slowly forward on to his face with a thud.

'Oh dear,' Raven said, 'it appears you have just shot your friend.' She lifted the already broken arm again and the invisible man screamed in pain and dropped his gun. Raven ripped his mask off with her free hand.

'Now you're going to tell me who you work for,' she said as she pushed the crippled man away from her and drew the other sword from her back, 'or you, my friend, are going to experience some very, very dramatic weight loss.'

☢☢☢

'Please, I am having to stop, just for a minute,' Franz said, leaning against a tree and breathing heavily. It was really dark now, especially deep within the forest. They were forced to move more slowly as it became more difficult to pick out a path through the trees in the gloom.

'No, we should keep moving,' Wing said. 'Our pursuers will have little difficulty tracking us through this terrain.'

'Two minutes,' Otto said, 'everybody take a breath but we can't stop for any longer. Wing's right, we have to try to get to the mountains by nightfall. We need to find shelter.' Otto knew full well that this was not a part of the world where you wanted to be outdoors at night if you could help it. The only consolation was that the same would also be true for their pursuers.

'Who do you think attacked us?' Tom asked, sitting down on the trunk of a fallen tree.

'I have no idea,' Otto said, shaking his head, 'but whoever it is they're unusually well equipped. That helicopter gunship was state of the art and its on-board systems were shielded against my abilities. I'll tell you one thing though, they're certainly not amateurs.'

'Do you think any of the other Alphas escaped?' Laura asked.

'I don't know,' Otto replied. 'I hope so.'

The others continued to rest for a minute as Otto walked over to Wing who stood silently watching the forest in the direction they'd just come from.

'You see something?' Otto asked, searching for any sign of movement amongst the trees.

'No,' Wing replied with a frown, 'but something is not right. We should get going.'

☻☻☻

The commander of the Disciple assault team watched as the last of the captured Alpha students were forced on to the heavy transport helicopter. A few seconds later the twin rotors of the giant machine began to slowly rotate. He turned his back and walked towards the other transport that the rest of his men were boarding. His earpiece emitted a soft bleep and he tapped it once to receive the incoming communication.

'Go ahead,' the commander said, raising his voice over the noise of the transport's thumping rotor blades.

'Sir, we've found the men who were sent to retrieve Raven's body,' the voice on the other end reported. Those men had been sent out an hour ago and had not checked in. The commander had despatched another team to

188

investigate. 'They're both dead. One was shot and the other appears to have been killed with an edged weapon.'

'She's alive,' the commander said angrily. 'Get back here, we need to move to the rendezvous point before G.L.O.V.E.'s forces arrive.'

'Roger that,' the soldier on the other end replied.

The commander hurried over to the other side of the clearing where the crew were watching the last of the missiles being removed from their helicopter gunships.

'I need you in the air now,' the commander said to one of the pilots. 'Raven is somewhere out there and I need eyes in the sky.'

'Wheels-up in five minutes,' one of the pilots replied.

'Good, the rendezvous point is set up and ready. Return there to refuel and rearm when necessary.'

'Understood,' the pilot replied with a nod.

The commander switched channels on his communicator and waited for a second as the device connected.

'This is Minerva, go ahead,' the voice on the other end said.

'It appears that Raven survived the destruction of her aircraft,' the commander replied slightly nervously. The Disciples were notoriously intolerant of failure and the consequences for disappointing them were always harsh.

'I see,' Minerva said calmly. 'I did warn you that she would prove to be a more challenging kill than you expected. We have lost the element of surprise. She will be considerably more difficult to eliminate now.'

'Should we abort?' the commander asked.

'Certainly not. I said she would be difficult to eliminate commander, not impossible,' Minerva said impatiently. 'Do you have any idea of her current location?'

'No, but I believe she will attempt to rendezvous with the group of H.I.V.E. students that we're currently tracking,' the commander said.

'Good, if she meets up with them it will make her much easier to track,' Minerva replied. 'She will not abandon them and we will use that fact to our full advantage.'

☻☻☻

Otto jogged along beside Wing as they struggled to pick out a path through the forest in the darkness. The other Alphas followed, some finding the demanding pace that Wing was setting easier to maintain than others.

'I am thinking I am having the heart attack,' Franz said, his face red with exertion.

'Hey, this is good exercise,' Shelby said with a grin. 'I don't know about anyone else but I'm really starting to feel the burn here.'

'I am still hoping to be avoiding the burning,' Franz replied breathlessly, 'and the shooting and the stabbing and the strangling and . . .'

'OK, Franz, we get the idea,' Nigel gasped.

Wing suddenly stopped.

'What is it?' Otto whispered.

Wing cocked his head to one side, as if listening to something.

'Everybody get down!' Wing yelled, pushing Otto to the floor. The Alphas dropped to the ground just a split second before the forest behind them exploded with the sound of gunfire, lighting up with muzzle flashes. Otto scrambled to cover behind a tree as bullets buzzed through the air all around him. He looked for Wing but his friend was nowhere to be seen.

'Hold your fire,' a voice shouted and the gunfire stopped immediately. 'Surrender now – you have nowhere to run. The next time we open fire we will not miss.'

The leader of the Disciple tracking team studied the heat signatures of the children who were lying on the ground or hiding behind trees thirty metres away. The night vision system in his suit's mask was good but it was impossible to tell at this range which one was Otto Malpense. His instructions had been clear: once he had Malpense the other H.I.V.E. students were to be eliminated.

'Last chance,' he yelled, 'three, two . . .'

Wing struck without mercy, silently dropping from the trees overhead, and delivering a scything chop to the squad leader's throat. The man emitted a strangled gurgling sound as he dropped his assault rifle and clutched at his throat. Wing ripped the soldier's mask off as he collapsed to the ground. He pulled the mask on and the previously invisible soldiers lit up in front of him, five of them in a tight group, their backs turned.

'Sorry, boss, didn't get that. What did you say?' one of the other men in the squad said, turning his head. He just had time for a frightened yelp as he saw the figure leaping towards him. Wing grabbed the barrel of the man's rifle as it swung towards him and wrenched it upwards, the shoulder rest smashing into the soldier's chin and knocking him clean off his feet. Wing kept moving, swinging the rifle like a hammer into the ribs of another soldier, while delivering a vicious kick to the side of his knee. As the crippled man dropped to the ground, screaming in pain, Wing swung the rifle into the side of his head, knocking him out cold. There was a burst of panic fire from one of the other men as Wing dived for cover, rolling towards the nearest one of the Disciple troops who was still standing. He leapt up, driving the heel of his palm into the man's nose, shattering the bones with a crunch. The man squeezed the trigger of his gun instinctively and the wild shots cut down one of his own team-mates. Wing delivered a backhanded fist to the side of the gunman's head, dropping him like a stone. Wing spun towards the last remaining uninjured member of the squad but the Disciple soldier had him cold, his rifle aimed straight at Wing's head.

His finger was tightening on the trigger as, from nowhere, a glowing purple blade flashed through the air. The rifle dropped to the ground as the soldier toppled over, about a foot shorter than he had been just a moment before.

'I am relieved to see you are unharmed,' Wing said calmly.

'Likewise Mr Fanchu,' Raven replied with a nod.

Otto and the others slowly began to emerge from cover as Wing and Raven walked towards them.

'I had a feeling we hadn't seen the last of you,' Otto said with a grin.

'Six hours and thirteen minutes,' Raven said, looking at her watch. 'Looks like my twenty-four hour record is safe. To be honest, I was expecting slightly better from this group.'

'Very funny,' Otto said. 'I don't suppose you have a plan for getting us out of here alive, do you?'

'Yes, first we take anything that might be useful from our friends back there,' Raven replied, gesturing towards the battered remnants of the Disciple tracking team. 'Then, we run.'

'I was being afraid you were going to say that,' Franz moaned.

☻☻☻

'Come in, Frostbite Three,' the commander of the Disciple troops said urgently into his communicator but there was no reply. They had lost contact with the tracking team half an hour ago and there been no communication since. They were the last of his troops equipped with the new camouflage suits which were supposed to make them undetectable and he was starting to worry that something had happened to them. He had dispatched his helicopter gunships to the scene but they would soon have to return to base if the winter storm that they were flying through continued to develop.

'We're nearly at the rendezvous point,' the pilot of the transport helicopter reported. 'ETA two minutes.'

The commander nodded and headed back into the cargo compartment of the chopper. Inside were a dozen of his men. They had been trained by the best and they were extremely well equipped but he had started to wonder if that would be enough. Raven and the remaining H.I.V.E. students were proving to be difficult, dangerous prey.

'We're heading to the secondary staging area,' the commander said. 'We will rest overnight there and restart the search for our remaining targets in the morning. This storm should have blown itself out by then. It is likely that, by then, there will be G.L.O.V.E. forces in the area searching for their people. If you encounter them you are cleared to engage.'

'I assume *she's* still out there, sir,' one of his men asked.

'Yes, we believe that Raven is still active,' the commander replied. 'You have all been briefed on her capabilities. I'm sure that I do not need to remind you of the threat she represents. Do not engage her without backup.'

'There's a transmission coming in for you, commander,' the pilot shouted back from the cockpit. The commander tapped his earpiece.

'This is Frostbite One, go ahead.'

'Good evening, commander,' Minerva replied. 'I hear you have lost contact with one of your tracking teams.'

'Yes, I'd like to call off the search for Raven and the H.I.V.E students for the night. This storm is too intense for airborne operations and visibility on the ground will be no better. The weather should have improved by the morning and we can relaunch the search then.'

'Very well,' Minerva replied. 'I too will be arriving at the rendezvous point in the morning.'

'You're coming here?' The commander asked, sounding surprised.

'Yes,' Minerva said. 'I want to make sure that you and your men are sufficiently . . . motivated.'

'Understood,' the commander said, swallowing nervously. 'We will prepare for your arrival.'

☻☻☻

'Up there,' Raven shouted over the howling wind. She pointed towards a darkened hollow in the mountainside above them, barely visible through the increasingly heavy snow. 'We have to find shelter. This storm is going to get worse before it gets better.'

The Alphas followed behind her as she picked her way carefully up the rocky slope. The trees were thinner here and provided less protection from the freezing wind. Even with their specially adapted environmental suits it was getting unbearably cold. They were exhausted but knew that they could not stop until they'd found a safe place to rest. Raven reached the mouth of the cave and peered inside. She pulled a glowstick from her tactical harness and lit it up, bending it until the glass tube inside cracked and then shaking it to mix the phosphorescent chemicals. Pulling one of the swords from her back she advanced into the cave with the glowing stick held high, the eerie green light from the plastic tube casting unsettling shadows on the walls as she went deeper. The cave went much further back than it had seemed it would from the outside. By the time they reached the back of the cave the sound of the howling wind outside was little more than a distant moan.

'We should be safe here,' Raven said, sticking the light in a small recess in one of the rocky walls. The tired Alphas leant the rifles they had taken from the Disciple soldiers against the wall before finding places to rest on the gravel-strewn floor.

'We can't risk a fire, I'm afraid,' Raven said. 'Not that we could gather firewood in this blizzard anyway. Just stay close to one another to conserve your body heat and you'll be fine.'

'Who were those guys?' Otto asked as Raven sat down nearby.

'Old friends of ours,' Raven replied. 'The Disciples.'

'I was hoping we'd seen the last of them when Overlord was destroyed,' Wing said with a frown.

'It would seem not,' Raven said.

'Did any of the other Alphas escape?' Laura asked.

'I don't know,' Raven said, looking at the ground, 'but the initial missile attack on the other Shrouds was . . . some may have survived, but many will not. I fear our casualties will be heavy. This was a well-planned ambush. God only knows how they found out where the Hunt was taking place. Only Nero, H.I.V.E.mind and myself knew the location. All I can think is that they managed to track the G.L.O.V.E. Hunt team here somehow but I don't see how.'

'So what do we do now?' Penny asked.

'We stay here overnight and hope that this storm breaks,' Raven replied. 'Then we make ourselves as easy for H.I.V.E. to find as possible.'

'You mean head back to the landing site?' Nigel asked, looking confused.

'No,' Raven replied, 'too risky. Besides, we don't need to.' She reached into one of the pockets on her tactical harness and pulled out a small metal box. 'We have this.'

'What is it?' Otto asked.

'It's the homing beacon from the ejector seat that I used to escape the Shroud before it was destroyed. It's supposed to help with locating downed pilots but we can use it too. It won't activate again until I reattach the battery but when I do it will give H.I.V.E. our exact position.'

'So why haven't you activated it?' Shelby asked with a frown.

'Because it will tell *everyone* else exactly where we are,' Otto said. 'Right?'

'Exactly,' Raven nodded. 'We need to find somewhere we can hole up, some kind of fortified position, before we activate it. When we do we'll be broadcasting our location to the Disciples too so we have to find somewhere that will allow us to hold them off until H.I.V.E.'s forces can get to us.'

'OK, so where do we go?' Shelby asked.

'There's an abandoned Russian army training base on the other side of these mountains,' Raven said. 'I'm not sure exactly what kind of facility it was but it's probably the best option if we want to make a stand.'

'And then we just hope that H.I.V.E. gets to us before the ammunition runs out,' Otto said, gesturing towards the rifles stacked against the wall.

'Great,' Shelby said, 'nothing I like more than a hopeless last stand against overwhelming odds.'

'Way to boost morale, Shel,' Laura groaned.

'Sorry, what I meant to say was that it's a brilliant plan and I don't see how it can possibly fail.'

'Somehow, that's actually worse,' Nigel said with a sigh.

'OK, try to get some sleep,' Raven said. 'We have a long climb tomorrow. I'll keep watch.'

He knew he wouldn't be able to sleep. There was a problem that had been nagging at him and something that Raven said had made it bubble back to the surface. Only she, Nero and H.I.V.E.mind had known about the location for the Hunt but Otto knew that wasn't entirely true. Everyone in the cave had known. As he looked at his friends settling down to try and get a few hours' sleep he realised something horrible. There was only one explanation that made any sense. Someone here had sold them out. One of his friends was a traitor.

☻☻☻

The following morning Otto woke with a start. What little sleep he'd managed to get had been plagued by nightmares. Raven was still watching the entrance to the cave through which the grey light of dawn was now visible.

'Good morning,' she said quietly.

'How's the weather?' Otto asked, slowly getting to his feet. He felt stiff and uncomfortable after the night spent on the rocky floor of the cave.

'Much improved,' Raven replied. 'We should be able to set out for the abandoned facility shortly.'

'I'll wake up the others,' Otto said.

A few minutes later the Alphas were all awake and getting ready for the trek that lay ahead of them.

'I'm starving,' Tom moaned. 'I suppose it was too much to ask that one of those Disciple soldiers might have been carrying some rations.'

'I believe that part of the challenge of the Hunt was that we were to find our own sources of food,' Wing said, 'though I concede that foraging probably isn't very wise under the circumstances.'

'I am thinking that I am actually being too frightened to be hungry,' Franz sighed.

'OK, that's it, we're doomed,' Shelby whispered to Laura.

'There are five rifles left,' Raven said, slinging one of the salvaged weapons over her shoulder. 'So three of you will have to remain unarmed. Wing, I know you won't take one even if I tell you to so I need two more volunteers.'

'I'll pass,' Penny said. 'I've never fired a gun in my life. I'd probably only end up shooting myself.'

'I don't need one either,' Laura said. 'I'm no good with the damn things anyway.'

The other five Alphas all took one of the rifles. Tom picked one up and gave Otto an embarrassed look.

'I don't suppose you've got a minute to . . . erm . . . show me the basics have you?' he asked quietly.

'Sure,' Otto said, 'it's a piece of cake really. Safety's here, white dot means that the safety's on, red dot means it's off. Best to leave it on until you're ready to shoot. Sights are here – just make sure that you keep whatever you want to hit in the middle of them but never point your weapon at anything you don't want to kill. Keep your finger outside the trigger guard until you want to pull the trigger. I've been chewed out too many times by Colonel Francisco for bad trigger discipline to forget that. Right, OK, pull the stock tight into your shoulder. That's it. It will kick a bit so lean into the rifle as you squeeze the trigger. Squeeze, not pull, gently does it. Try to use short controlled bursts of fire – you haven't got enough ammo for spray and pray. OK?'

'How do you know all this?' Tom asked, looking at Otto with a slightly bemused expression.

'Benefits of a good education,' Otto replied with a smile.

'OK, time to go,' Raven said. 'Keep together and keep up.'

☻☻☻

Nero stared at the satellite image of the Hunt base camp as Francisco's assault Shroud touched down. Two more hovered nearby, scanning the area for any sign of hostile

201

forces. Nero watched the Colonel's men move around the wreckage-strewn site.

'It's bad, Max,' Francisco said over the comms system. 'There are a lot of bodies. All the pilots and security personnel are dead and we've found nearly twenty dead students. The others are all missing. Raven's Shroud seems to have escaped the initial attack at least. We're going to sweep the area and see if we can find any sign of it.'

'Damn it!' Nero shouted, slamming his palm down on the display. 'Colonel, I want you to find the people responsible for this atrocity and I want you to make sure they suffer before they die. Do I make myself clear?'

'It will be my pleasure,' Francisco replied. 'We're going to start our search immediately but it's going to take some time. There's a lot of territory to cover.'

'Report anything you find,' Nero said angrily.

'Understood, Francisco out.'

'H.I.V.E.mind, begin scanning the satellite imagery of the surrounding area,' Nero snapped. 'Look for something that might give us an idea where these people are or where they may have taken any survivors.'

Nero stood in the middle of the control room and felt pure rage welling up inside him.

'Summon the ruling council,' Nero barked at a nearby communications technician. 'Tell them I will be sending

Shrouds to pick them up immediately for an emergency meeting at H.I.V.E.'

If it was war that the Disciples wanted, it was war they were going to get.

chapter ten

Otto tried to ignore the freezing wind as he pulled himself up towards the next handhold. He was also trying very hard to ignore the fact that there were no safety lines protecting him from the increasingly long drop to the jagged rocks below. In fact, Otto thought, there were all sorts of things that he would rather ignore at the moment, given the choice. Above him Raven, Wing and Shelby were picking their way up the rock face with an ease and grace that made the rest of them look clumsy.

'I suppose it's pointless to ask them to slow down,' Penny said as she hauled herself up alongside Otto.

'I think the idea is that we go faster,' Otto replied.

'Oh, I could go much faster,' Laura said. 'All I have to do is let go. OK, I'd be travelling in the wrong direction but I'd be going really, really fast.'

'Not for very long though,' Otto replied with a grin. 'In

fact, I think you might find that eventually you'll come to a rather sudden stop.'

'I am being glad that everyone is finding the idea of us being plummeting to our doom so highly amusing,' Franz moaned.

'Franz, I thought we agreed not to use the word "plummeting" again until we reached the top,' Nigel said.

'Ah, yes, sorry.'

Otto looked upwards and saw Shelby pulling herself on to a wide ledge beside Wing and Raven.

'Come on, guys,' Otto said. 'Just a few metres then we can rest.'

A minute later Otto pulled himself over the edge of the outcropping and stood up. They were now a couple of hundred metres above the cave they had sheltered in overnight and the view back down into the valley was impressive. Raven stood silently looking out across the valley.

'See anyth—' Otto began to ask before Raven raised a single finger to her lips.

'Listen,' she whispered.

At first Otto couldn't hear anything over the wind but then very faintly he began to pick up another sound – the distant, regular thump of rotor blades.

'Everybody on to the ledge quickly,' Raven shouted as the last stragglers scaled the final few metres. 'Get down.'

They all lay down as the sound of the helicopter got louder and louder. A minute later they watched as a helicopter flew into the valley below at low altitude. The helicopter landed on the valley floor and a dozen men in white poured out of its rear hatch. The Alphas all knew who it was they were trying to find.

'Well, that can't be good,' Shelby said quietly.

'We have to keep climbing,' Raven said, watching the Disciple troops fanning out across the valley floor below. 'It won't take them long to find our trail and I don't want to get caught halfway up the side of a mountain by that helicopter. Let's go.'

'I've got a really bad feeling about this,' Laura whispered to Otto as Raven stepped up to the rock face and began to climb again.

'Well, you know what they say about being at your lowest point,' Otto replied.

'What?'

Otto looked at her and then up the mountainside.

'The only way is up.'

☻☻☻

The squad leader of the Disciple search team walked up the steep slope to the cave that one of his men had found a few minutes earlier. Still clearly visible in the snow around the cave mouth were several sets of footprints. He followed the trail for a few hundred metres and it ended at the base of a steep rock face. He looked upwards and for an instant thought he saw something moving. He pulled the binoculars from his belt and looked through them, scanning the rock face. There, clearly visible now, were several figures dressed in black climbing up the mountainside.

'Tell our sniper that I want him back on the transport chopper and in the air,' he said to one of his men. 'I have some target practice for him.'

☻☻☻

Raven pulled herself over the edge of the plateau and looked back down into the valley. She could barely make out the shapes of the men searching for them far below but what she could see were the rotors on the transport helicopter starting to spin. Within just a few seconds the chopper began to slowly lift into the air.

'Quickly,' she said, taking Shelby's hand and pulling her up. Wing climbed up beside them as the helicopter started to ascend rapidly towards them. 'They've spotted us.'

'Guys, come on,' Shelby yelled down to the others, who were twenty metres below and still climbing. 'We've got company!'

Otto glanced over his shoulder and immediately wished he hadn't. There was a helicopter a couple of hundred metres away at the same height as them. He began to climb again, as quickly as he could. Above him Raven unslung the assault rifle from her back and aimed at the helicopter's cockpit. She fired a three-round burst that left a series of spiderweb cracks across the curved plexiglas and the pilot tipped the transport away from the mountainside. Raven lowered her rifle as Shelby raised hers.

'Don't bother,' Raven said as the helicopter dropped back into a stationary hover a thousand metres away. 'That pilot knows what he's doing, they're out of range.'

The side door of the transport chopper slid open and a few seconds later there was a flash from inside. A moment later there was a buzzing sound and a tiny cloud of dirt was kicked up at Shelby's feet.

'Get down,' Raven snapped as there was another muzzle flash inside the distant helicopter and a bullet whined past Wing's ear. The three of them dropped to the ground as it struck the edge of the plateau.

'I thought you said they were out of range,' Shelby yelled as a shot hit the ground just a few centimetres in front of her.

'They are,' Raven said. 'Unfortunately we're not.'

Whoever was firing at them from the helicopter was obviously armed with a high-powered sniper rifle with a much greater effective range than the assault rifles they were carrying. They were far enough out that it would still be hard for the sniper to hit anything with real precision, especially from a moving platform, but they would get lucky eventually.

Otto reached for his next handhold. The rock just to his right splintered with a crack as a bullet smacked into it.

'Keep moving,' Raven yelled from above. 'Remember you're just an easier target if you freeze up.'

'Easy for her to say,' Penny muttered under her breath, hauling herself towards the top.

'Come on, Franz,' Nigel said, grabbing his friend's hand and pulling him upwards.

'I am being climbing as fast as I can!' Franz shouted.

'I know, but we have to get to the . . .'

Nigel gasped in surprise as the bullet hit him in the shoulder. He slowly tipped backwards away from the rock face and fell. Franz caught him with one hand, his knuckles turning white as they clamped on to Nigel's collar. Franz clung desperately to the rock with his other hand as another bullet struck nearby sending stinging stone splinters into his face.

'HELP!' Franz yelled.

'We have to help them,' Otto shouted up to Wing, Raven and Shelby.

'Follow my lead,' Raven said, detaching one of the grappler units from her forearm and throwing it to Wing. He quickly strapped it on to his wrist and watched as Raven fired the bolt into the ground at the edge of the drop-off at the edge of the plateau. Wing did the same and then chased after her as she ran back away from the edge, the monofilament from the grapplers trailing out behind them as they went.

'Lock your line,' Raven said, hitting the control on her own grappler. 'OK, follow me.'

Otto and Penny pulled themselves up and over the edge just in time to see Raven sprint towards them and launch herself over the edge of the drop-off with Wing just two steps behind her. They both flew outwards before dropping and swinging back in towards the rock face below as the grappler lines went tight. Raven hit the rocks just to the right of Nigel and Franz and Wing landed on the other side. Raven swung closer and wrapped her free arm around Nigel's waist.

'Franz, let go!' Raven shouted as a bullet whined past her head. 'I've got him.'

Franz slowly released his white-knuckled grip on Nigel's collar as Raven took the wounded boy's weight.

'Wing, get Franz up there,' Raven shouted as she pulled Nigel closer and hit the trigger on her grappler, reeling in the line and rocketing up the side of the mountain.

'Come on!' Wing shouted to Franz, wrapping an arm around his waist. Franz put one arm around Wing's neck and gripped on to his collar. Wing hit the trigger and reeled them both in, sending them shooting upwards as a bullet struck the rocks precisely where they had been hanging just a moment before.

Otto helped Wing and Franz back over the edge as bullets continued to kick up plumes of dirt from the ground around them. Moments later Laura and Tom clambered on to the plateau too as Raven and Shelby dragged Nigel back away from the edge.

Suddenly Penny hissed in pain as another one of the sniper's bullets found its mark. She staggered forward before falling to the ground, clutching her thigh.

'We have to find cover!' Raven shouted, hauling Nigel away from the edge as Otto and Tom ran over to Penny. They picked her up, an arm over each of their shoulders as more rounds buzzed through the air nearby.

'Franz! What are you doing?' Laura shouted as Franz unslung the rifle from his back and walked back towards the edge of the cliff.

'I am having just about enough of you,' Franz muttered under his breath as he raised the rifle and sighted. 'This is for hurting my friend.' He fired one short burst and then another.

'Don't waste your ammo,' Raven yelled as she continued to drag the unconscious Nigel away from the cliff. 'You'll never hit them from here.'

Suddenly black smoke started to billow out of the engine

cowling on the distant helicopter and it began to slowly spin down towards the valley below.

'Well, I'll be damned,' Shelby said. 'Dibs on getting to tell Colonel Francisco about this if we ever make it back to H.I.V.E.'

'How is Nigel being?' Franz asked as he slung the rifle on his back and walked over to Raven who had unzipped Nigel's environmental suit and was inspecting the wound in his shoulder.

'It could be worse,' Raven said as she pulled a field dressing from one of the pouches on her tactical harness. 'That was an excellent shot, Mr Argentblum.'

'That is not being important,' Franz said, shaking his head. 'What is being important is that Nigel and Penny are OK.'

'Otto, use this,' Raven said, throwing another dressing pack to him. Otto ripped open the pack and began to wrap the bandage inside tightly around the wound in Penny's thigh. Otto could see through the tear in the leg of her suit that she had been lucky – the bullet had just grazed her.

'Don't worry,' Otto said as Penny hissed in pain. 'It's just a flesh wound. Not much more than a scratch really.'

'Oh, I am sorry that my first gunshot wound isn't terribly impressive,' Penny said with a pained smile. 'I'll try to do better for you next time.'

'I think I'd rather avoid there being a next time actually,' Tom said frowning.

Franz, Laura and Shelby watched as Raven finished dressing Nigel's wound.

'Is he going to be OK?' Laura asked, sounding worried.

'I think so but we should still try to get him medical attention as quickly as possible. It looks like a clean wound, the bullet went straight through, but I can't be certain that there are no internal injuries. We need to get to the facility and activate the beacon as soon as possible.'

A moment later Nigel's eyes slowly opened and he looked up at his friends.

'What happened?' he asked, sounding groggy.

'You got shot by a sniper and fell off a mountain, Franz and Raven saved you from certain death and then Franz shot down a helicopter,' Shelby said with a grin.

'No really,' Nigel said with a frown, 'tell me, what happened?'

☺☹☺

The Alphas trudged through the snow towards the pair of huge rusted metal doors set in the side of the mountain. They had been following the crumbling remains of a disused road for the past twenty minutes. It was the first sign of human habitation that any of them had seen since they had arrived in Siberia and Otto felt that there was something vaguely sinister about it. What was it exactly that the Russian army would have been so keen to keep hidden away out here?

'So you don't have any idea what this place is?' Otto asked Raven as they walked past the collapsed remains of a military gatepost.

'No,' Raven replied. 'Something the authorities wanted to keep hidden obviously but, beyond that, your guess is as good as mine.'

'How do we know it's not a nuclear weapons dump?' Laura asked, eyeing the heavy doors with suspicion. 'For all we know this place could be radioactively contaminated.'

'Do you have a Geiger counter on you?' Raven asked.

'Err . . . no,' Laura replied.

'Well then, I shouldn't worry about it,' Raven said with a crooked smile.

In the centre of the doors was a large spoked wheel that was clearly supposed to be rotated to release the huge metal locking bars that bolted the door shut. In the middle of the wheel was an odd, star-shaped keyhole.

'I'm guessing that nobody has a key, right?' Shelby said with a smile. 'Come on then, out of the way, let's have a look at it.'

The others stepped aside and Shelby began to examine the lock. Penny sat down on a low concrete wall nearby and gently rubbed her wounded thigh as Franz helped Nigel sit down beside her. He was pale and they could all see from his expression that he was in considerable pain.

'OK,' Shelby said after a couple of minutes, 'anyone bring any plastic explosives?'

'Oh, great,' Otto said with a sigh.

'Just kidding,' Shelby grinned. 'I am going to need one of those though.' Shelby pointed at one of the silver cylinders on Raven's tactical harness.

'Wouldn't it be easier to just cut our way in?' Laura asked, pointing to the katanas strapped to Raven's back. 'Those things can cut through anything, right?'

'That would make it rather difficult to secure the door again from the inside,' Raven replied, handing Shelby one of her flashbang grenades. 'Though I'm struggling to see how this will help.'

'Oh ye of little faith,' Shelby said, pulling the pin from the grenade and handing it to Otto. 'Don't let go of that.'

'Oh, thank you very much,' Otto said, keeping a tight hold on the spring-loaded safety lever.

'Right then,' Shelby said, turning back to the lock, 'let's crack this puppy.'

She straightened the loop at the end of the safety pin and then made a series of tiny intricate bends at the other end.

'Oh, that's just beautiful,' Tom said admiringly as he watched Shelby work. 'I've seen the Maxwell twist before but I never realised that you could combine it with a reverse Mahler helix. That's brilliant.'

'You know, I'm really starting to like you,' Shelby said with a grin as she slid the newly created pick into the lock. She closed her eyes and slowly twisted the pick.

'You do know that you stick your tongue out when you're doing that, don't you?' Otto said.

'Seriously, Malpense?' Shelby said, eyes still closed. 'Now you start with the distracting banter?'

'Sorry,' Otto said, 'it's just that I get nervous when I'm holding live explosive devices.'

'Shhh, just let Aunty Shelby work her . . . magic!' There was a click and Shelby stepped back from the lock. 'A round of applause might be nice, you know.'

'Don't,' Laura said as Tom raised his hands to clap. 'You'll just encourage her.'

Wing stepped forward, gripped the spokes of the wheel and turned, the large metal locking bolts screeching in protest as they released in a shower of rust. He pushed hard and the massive doors slowly swung inwards with a pained creaking sound. Raven cracked another glowstick and walked slowly into the darkness beyond the doors.

'Last one into the creepy, dark, possibly radioactive abandoned military facility is a loser,' Shelby said as she followed Raven inside.

Colonel Francisco walked towards the burnt-out wreckage of the missing Shroud that was scattered across the valley floor.

'We've found the pilot and co-pilot's bodies but there's no sign of Raven or the students who were on-board,' one of the G.L.O.V.E. troops reported as Francisco approached.

'You're certain?'

'Yes, sir, we've done a full scan of the wreckage. It seems that the Shroud was hit while it was on the ground. One of the ejector seats is missing too. It looks like Raven and the passengers have either been captured or they somehow managed to escape.'

'Spread out and search for any signs of survivors,' Francisco said to the rest of the troops. 'We need to know what happened here.'

Francisco continued walking through the debris field. Lying not too far from the Shroud were the twisted remains of a helicopter rotor blade. Someone had clearly managed to take down at least one of the enemy helicopters. The question was how? The transport Shrouds had no weapons. Something about the whole scene just didn't make sense.

'Over here,' one of the G.L.O.V.E. troops yelled.

Francisco hurried over to where the man was standing and found two dead bodies lying just inside the forest. Both were wearing white thermoptic camouflage suits.

'Where did they get these from?' Francisco said, kneeling

217

down beside one of the dead men. The technology behind the suits' holographic projection cloak was one of G.L.O.V.E.'s most closely guarded secrets. The fact that it had somehow fallen into the Disciples' hands was deeply worrying. One of the men had been shot but the other man had been killed with a blade. The edges of the fatal wound were cauterised as if the blade had been heated or . . . Francisco suddenly realised what weapon might have caused a wound like that. He looked at the ground around the two bodies and saw several sets of tracks leading further into the forest.

'I want the search continued along that vector,' he said, pointing into the trees. 'We may have survivors in need of assistance.'

He pulled his communicator from his belt and thumbed the transmit button.

'Go ahead, Colonel,' Nero responded.

'Max, I think Raven's alive and even better, she may not be the only survivor.'

☁ ☁ ☁

Shelby locked the massive doors from the inside and handed the improvised key to Otto.

'There you go,' she said with a smile. 'Gee, I hope you can get the pin back in the grenade what with the pin being bent now and all.'

'You know you really are hilarious,' Otto replied, as he forced the safety pin back into the grenade. 'Truly, side-splittingly funny. I hope that nothing bad happens to you because then who would make sure that I'm always in such a constant state of intense amusement?'

'If you two are quite finished,' Raven said, taking the grenade from Otto and reattaching it to her tactical harness, 'I'm quite keen to find out what sort of facility we've actually locked ourselves inside.'

Raven walked down the darkened corridor ahead of the Alphas, the green light from her glowstick doing little to diminish the creepiness of the long dark corridor. Water dripped from the ceiling, pooling on the floor. They passed several doors that led to empty locker rooms and barracks with rows of rusty iron bunks.

'Zombies,' Penny said. 'I mean, just look at this place. There's definitely going to be zombies.'

'I am thinking this but I am wishing that you are not saying it, yes?' Franz said quietly.

'Whatever this place is no one's been here for a *loooong* time,' Otto said.

'Except the zombies,' Shelby said.

'Obviously, except the zombies.'

'Please be stopping it,' Franz said plaintively.

Soon they came to another heavy metal door but this one was not locked. As Raven pushed it open dim, grey light came from the other side. The room beyond was lined with control panels on three sides but the fourth was a panel of dirty glass that looked out on to a massive cavern. Set in the glass was a door that led out on to a gantry running round the walls of the cavern. Daylight streamed down from an opening somewhere overhead, but what was truly bizarre was spread across the cavern floor. As they all walked on to the gantry they looked down on to an impossible scene from the past. Laid out before them was a perfect recreation of a small American town from the early1960s. There was a diner, a drugstore, a church and even what looked like a fire station in the town square. Surrounding the centre were acres of suburban homes and schools. It was exactly as if somebody had picked up an entire American town fifty years ago and then dropped it in a cavern in Siberia. The only slightly incongruous detail were the abandoned Russian military vehicles that were dotted around the town. Far overhead was a huge geodesic glass dome that allowed the daylight to shine through. Some of its triangular panels were missing but otherwise it was intact.

'OK, you know what,' Otto said, 'I wasn't expecting that.'

'On the plus side, it isn't zombies,' Penny said, unable to take her eyes off the bizarre sight. 'Although that might actually have been marginally less weird.'

'Why on earth would anyone build this?' Laura asked.

'Training,' Raven said. 'I'd heard rumours about places like this but I'd always thought it was a myth. Back in the early sixties there were people in the Russian military who were convinced that a war with America was not just probable but inevitable. That being the case, they had to find a way to train their men for an invasion but they had no towns that bore any resemblance to small-town America so they built places like this. I suppose it's not a myth any more.'

'Well, it may not be a myth any more,' Otto said with a smile, 'but I'll tell you what it is. A really, really good place to hide.'

☢ ☢ ☢

The helicopter landed in the centre of the camp, the down draught from its rotor blades whipping clouds of snow into the air. A figure dressed in a long black hooded coat and a dark veil that covered her face stepped down from the side hatch and walked towards the commander. The commander swallowed nervously. The woman was Minerva and she had been the head of the Disciples ever since the disastrous events at the Advanced Weapons Project facility in Colorado that had resulted in Overlord's destruction. He had good reason to be nervous – she had a reputation for ruthlessness and little tolerance for failure.

'It is a pleasure to see you again, ma'am,' the commander said with a smart nod as the woman approached.

'Where are they?' Minerva asked.

'We're ... erm ... not certain at the moment,' the commander replied uncomfortably. 'One of our teams spotted them an hour ago climbing a mountain nearby but they were unable to neutralise them.'

'And you have not been able to locate them since?'

'No, we have sent gunships to the area but were unable to find them. It looks like they've gone to ground somewhere.'

'I am losing patience, commander,' Minerva said. 'You have had several chances to eliminate Raven and the last of Nero's brats and yet you seem to be incapable of finishing the job. This operation needs to be a success. We have to prove to Joseph Wright and the rest of the deposed G.L.O.V.E. leaders that they were right to forge an alliance with us. Don't make me regret putting you in charge of this operation – you should know that I am not in the habit of living with my regrets. Do I make myself clear?'

'Yes, ma'am,' the commander replied. 'I have tracker teams on the ground at their last known location. We will find them.'

'Let us hope so, commander, for your sake.'

Otto threw the switch and there was a slight vibration from somewhere beneath his feet as generators that had probably not been used for decades slowly rumbled into life.

'Gotta love Russian engineering,' he said to himself as the dusty control panels around the room began to light up. He moved to one of the panels nearer the window and threw another series of switches. Outside the control room, huge banks of floodlights on the walls lit up and flooded the cavern with light. Otto walked out on to the gantry and looked down on the fake town below. Now it was lit up it looked even more like some kind of impossibly elaborate movie set. He walked along the gantry and took the stairs down to the cavern floor where Raven and the rest of the Alphas were waiting.

'I can't believe that anything's still working,' Laura said as they walked through the town.

'They built things to last back then,' Raven said. 'Everything now is digital and fragile – when this place was built things were less sophisticated but they did not break quite so easily. Fortunately for us.'

'So what now?' Tom asked. 'Do we just activate the beacon and wait?'

'No, first we need to find good defensive positions,' Raven replied. 'We have to assume that the Disciples will get here before anyone from H.I.V.E. does. We also have to assume that they might find a way in here somehow.'

'There are plenty of places to hide here,' Laura said, looking around.

'I'm getting tired of hiding,' Otto said. 'I've got a better idea.'

'And what might that be?' Raven asked.

'Well, they say that offence is the best form of defence, right?' Otto said as they walked into the main town square.

'Normally I would agree,' Raven said, 'but the Disciples have us outnumbered and outgunned.'

'Not necessarily,' Otto said with a grin, pointing across the town square. 'It's like you said, some things are built to last.'

☢ ☢ ☢

'I think I've got something,' the radio operator in the Disciple command tent yelled.

'What is it?' the commander asked quickly.

'It sounds like a distress beacon of some kind,' the operator replied. 'I'm not entirely sure what the source of the transmission is but it's certainly not coming from any of our equipment.'

'It has to be Raven,' Minerva said. 'She's signalling for help. Can you determine the position of the transmitter?'

'Yes, it will take a few minutes but it should be relatively straightforward.'

'Good,' the commander said with a nod. 'Once you have a position relay the coordinates to the gunships and have them check the area.' He turned to Minerva. 'I'll get airborne with the rest of our troops so we can be on site as soon as we have the location.'

'I will accompany you,' Minerva said. 'I want to be there to personally ensure your success this time, commander.'

'But, ma'am, it could be extremely dangerous,' the commander protested.

'If I were you, commander, I would be more worried for the safety of your own troops. Raven must know that you will be able to trace the location of that beacon. It is no accident that she is telling you exactly where she is. Do not underestimate her or Nero's students. They are a dangerous combination, as Overlord discovered to his cost.'

'I know how dangerous they are,' the commander said, 'but she is only one woman and they are just children. We will not fail.'

☻☻☻

Cole Harrington sat in his cell in H.I.V.E.'s detention wing trying very hard not to think about what the future held for him. He had no idea how Otto Malpense had managed to transfer the stolen H.I.V.E.mind files to his Blackbox but he knew that whatever Nero might have in mind for him it would not be pleasant. He looked up as the door to his cell hissed open and Chief Dekker walked into the room.

'What do you want?' Harrington snapped bitterly. 'If it wasn't for you I wouldn't be in here.'

'Whatever do you mean?' Dekker asked with a smile.

'You're the one who told me what Malpense and those other Alphas were up to. You were the one who told me that you could sell H.I.V.E.mind's source code for so much money. It's because of you that I'm in this situation. Well, you're going to get me out of this somehow or I'm going to tell Nero all about your part in this. I'm not taking the fall for this alone.'

'You know, it's really very sad,' Dekker said, shaking her head.

'What are you talking about?'

'You obviously couldn't live with yourself after betraying H.I.V.E. so badly,' Dekker continued. 'You confessed everything to me, of course. How you'd found the proposed location for the Hunt amongst the files you stole from H.I.V.E.mind and then how you covertly transmitted the information to your contact. You even told me exactly where in your quarters you hid the covert transmitter that you had paid one of the security guards to smuggle into the school for you. During the course of my questioning I explained to you that the information you had unwittingly provided to the Disciples had been directly responsible for the massacre at the Hunt. You told me how you had no idea that anything like that would happen and that you desperately regretted your actions. Sadly you obviously just couldn't live with the guilt. If I'd realised that you were a suicide risk I would have kept a much closer watch on you. Such a shame.'

'Suicide? What do you mean suicide? I'd never . . . oh God no.'

Dekker walked towards him smiling nastily as the door hissed shut behind her.

chapter eleven

'Are you guys going to be OK in here?' Otto asked. He looked around the interior of the fake church and was struck by just how much attention to detail had been used when the building was constructed.

'Don't worry. We'll be fine,' Laura said, helping Tom lower Nigel on to the floor behind the altar.

'How are you feeling, Nigel?' Otto asked. His friend looked paler and his breathing seemed more laboured.

'I've felt better,' Nigel said quietly. 'I don't think I'd really recommend getting shot, to be honest.'

'It wasn't actually that high on my list of things to try,' Otto said with a smile. 'Don't worry, help will be here soon.'

Otto handed Laura one of the Disciple assault rifles.

'I know you don't want it but take it anyway. If they get past us, then it's up to you and Tom to protect Nigel and Penny.'

'Hey,' Penny said with a frown as she sat down next to Nigel, 'I'm not that badly hurt.'

'I know but you're not in any condition to go running around outside either,' Tom said. 'Don't worry, Otto, we'll be fine.'

'OK, I need to get back outside and make sure that Wing and Shel know what they're doing,' Otto said. 'See you guys soon.'

Otto and Laura walked back towards the church doors together. Otto pulled the door open but Laura pushed it shut and pulled him towards her.

'Good luck,' Laura said and then she kissed him. It felt just like he had hoped it would. It felt right. Otto pulled away from her and stared into her eyes. There was something there that he hadn't expected – she looked afraid.

'Hey, don't worry,' Otto said, 'we're going to get through this. In a few hours we'll all be back at H.I.V.E. wishing we had something more exciting to do.'

'I hope you're right,' Laura said with a sad smile.

''Course I'm right,' Otto said with a grin as he pushed the door open again. 'I always am, remember.'

☻☻☻

The Disciple commander examined the enormous rusted doors. There was no doubt that the beacon signal was coming from somewhere on the other side of them.

'The gunship's reporting that there's some sort of glass dome hidden between the peaks up there,' his comms officer said, pointing up to the rocky slopes that loomed above them. 'They're saying that there's some sort of artificial lighting inside and what look like buildings.'

'What is this place?' the commander asked with a frown. 'It's not on any of the maps.'

'That's not unusual for the Russian military,' the comms officer replied. 'At least that's who I'm assuming built this.'

'I want this door taken down,' the commander said. 'Get a demolition charge set up.'

'Yes, sir, it'll take a few minutes.'

The commander walked back down the road towards the two transport helicopters that had brought him and his troops up the mountain. Minerva waited as he approached.

'We should be inside shortly,' the commander reported.

'Good, the longer that beacon is transmitting the more likely it is that G.L.O.V.E. forces will detect it. We cannot afford a direct confrontation at this stage,' Minerva replied. 'Nero must be weakened first.'

Minerva and the commander watched as two of his men worked quickly to attach shaped charges to the metal door. After a couple of minutes they both hurried back towards the helicopters. The man holding the remote detonator looked at the commander and he gave a quick nod.

'Fire in the hole!'

'How did this happen?' Nero asked angrily. 'Why wasn't he searched more carefully when he was detained?'

He and Chief Dekker watched as two security guards carried a sheet-covered body on a stretcher out of the detention block.

'I'm sorry, Doctor Nero,' Dekker replied, 'it never occurred to me that he might have some sort of suicide capsule. It must have been smuggled to him by his Disciple contact. We know that they had equipment brought into the school for him by his contact. We found a covert transmitter hidden in his quarters. It seems that there was an awful lot about Cole Harrington that nobody knew.'

'What about his accomplices, the Henchman students?' Nero asked. 'Are they working for the Disciples as well?'

'No, I don't believe so,' Dekker replied. 'I think they were just unwitting pawns. In their case, very unwitting. I don't think either of them would even be able to spell "Disciple" much less leak information to them.'

'That still means that there is somebody inside the school who is working for the Disciples,' Nero said with a frown. 'It has to be somebody that has permission to leave the island or they wouldn't be able to get this equipment in the first place. Which means that we're either looking for a member of the teaching staff or someone on the support staff. Either way we're going to have to try and flush them out. We can't afford a traitor in our midst, especially at the moment.'

'I shall start conducting interviews with everyone who has been off the island in the last six months,' Dekker said. 'This isn't going to be easy. That's a lot of people when you consider how many of the teaching and support staff have taken leave during that period.'

'I suggest you start immediately, Chief. We have no time to lose.'

'Understood. I will schedule the first interviews for this afternoon.'

'Good. Now if you'll excuse me I'm going to head back to the control room to see if there have been any developments in the search for Raven and the surviving Alphas.'

Nero walked out of the detention centre and headed up the corridor towards the control room, his mind racing. Things were moving too fast. He was used to dealing with casualties in his line of work but he had never found it easy to accept the death of one of his students. The fact that the Disciples had murdered or captured almost an entire year of Alpha students was unbearable. Despite that, he knew that he had to stay focused. If he dwelled too much on the scale of the unfolding tragedy in Siberia he would be of no use to anyone. Raven and the remaining Alphas were still out there somewhere and he would do absolutely everything in his power to ensure that they were returned to the school unharmed. He walked into the control room and one of the communications technicians hurried over to him.

'Doctor Nero, we've just received a transmission from Colonel Francisco,' the tech said quickly. 'They've picked up a Shroud distress beacon in the mountains to the north of their current position. They're trying to get a fix on its location now.'

☣ ☣ ☣

The Disciple troops picked their way through the twisted remains of the metal doors in the mountainside and headed down the tunnel beyond with the commander and Minerva just behind them. Enough of the lights in the ceiling were working for them to see that this was clearly a military facility of some kind. There were rooms that were unmistakeably barracks and mess halls. The Disciple troops moved slowly and carefully, alert for any sign of booby traps or an ambush. They knew that they could take no chances, especially considering the prey that they were hunting. Eventually they arrived at the control room at the end of the passage. The soldiers took up defensive positions around the room as the commander and Minerva looked down through the huge window at the bizarre scene below them.

'A slice of apple pie in the heart of the motherland,' Minerva said. 'I had heard of such places existing but I had never seen one before today. I expect the Americans had an artificial Russian town just like this hidden away some-where too.'

'It may be a fascinating relic of the cold war,' the commander said, 'but it is also a problem. They could be anywhere down there.'

'Then I suggest you start your search immediately, commander,' Minerva replied. 'There is no time to waste.'

'OK. We'll head for the town square first,' the commander said, addressing his men, 'then conduct an expanding sweep search from there. Let's move out.'

The commander headed out on to the gantry and followed his men down the stairs to the cavern floor. They made slow but steady progress down the main street towards the centre of the town, checking carefully for any sign of a trap.

'How far to the beacon?' the commander asked as his men reached the town square.

'It seems to be coming from the church,' his comms officer replied, waving a small electronic device back and forth in front of him.

'OK, I want four-man fire teams there, there and there,' the commander said, pointing to positions around the outside of the square. 'Overlapping fields of fire. I want this square to be a kill box.'

His men moved quickly towards the strategic locations he had picked out. The commander knew that just because the beacon was in the church it didn't mean that Raven and the H.I.V.E. students would be but, he was certainly not going to take any chances at this stage. He needed to deactivate the beacon before G.L.O.V.E. could use it to pinpoint their location.

'OK, let's see if we can find that thing and turn it off,' the commander said. 'Ma'am, I suggest you wait here.'

Minerva gave a quick nod and the commander led the rest of his men across the square towards the church. They were halfway to the church when there was a monstrous roar from the direction of the fire station on the other side of the square. The commander and his men slowed, trying to identify where the sound was coming from. Suddenly, in an explosion of splintered wood, the doors on the front of the fire station's garage exploded outwards as a tank smashed through them.

Inside the tank Wing pressed hard on the accelerator pedal, sending the giant armoured vehicle roaring towards the startled group of soldiers in the middle of the square. The troops scattered in all directions as the tank bore down on them, a couple of them squeezing off pointless bursts of fire from their rifles, the rounds pinging harmlessly off the tank's armoured skin.

'Keep them away from the church,' Otto yelled from the command seat in the turret. Wing swung the tank towards the church doors, blocking the way as Otto brought the main gun to bear on one of the fire teams that the Disciples had set up at the edges of the square.

'Now, Shelby!' Otto yelled over the growl of the giant diesel engine. 'Fire!'

It had only taken Otto a minute to read the thick operations manual that he had found inside the tank, though it had taken slightly longer to try to show the others how the systems they would be operating worked. He doubted that any tank crew had been trained in half an hour before but thankfully it had been designed and engineered to actually be very straightforward to operate. What Otto was slightly less confident of was whether or not the fifty-year-old vehicle's main weapon was still functioning correctly.

'Woohoo!' Shelby yelled as she pulled the trigger on the main cannon's firing controls and the whole tank rocked with the recoil. On the far side of the square the building behind the Disciple troops' position exploded in a cloud of dust, shattered masonry and woodwork flying in all directions. Otto rotated the turret, towards one of the other Disciple positions. The men scattered, running for cover.

'Franz, give me a sitrep,' Otto said into the throat mic of one of the communicators that they had obtained from the soldiers in the woods the previous day. High above the square, in the church tower, Franz scanned the streets below with an ancient pair of binoculars which he had taken from the tank earlier.

'There is being one group heading down the road east of you,' Franz said as he watched the Disciple troops fleeing through the streets, trying to hide from the armoured monster that had suddenly attacked them. 'And there is being another group who are heading south towards where Raven is waiting.'

'OK, we're heading east,' Otto said, almost feeling sorry for the men who were fleeing south. 'Wing, take us through the drugstore.'

In one of the adjoining streets the commander led his men away from the square at a run. They were not equipped to take down a tank – they needed to retreat and regroup. He had seen other vehicles that had been left around the town during some long-forgotten military exercise but it had never occurred to him for a moment that there would be anything as deadly as a tank. Suddenly the ground beneath his feet began to tremble and then the tank exploded through the wall just in front of him, burying several of his men. He and the rest of his men turned and ran as the tank's turret rotated towards them. There was a thunderous boom and the wall ahead of them exploded. Several of his men went down as the commander ducked into an adjoining alleyway, running for his life.

To the south some of the remaining Disciple soldiers were gathered in the backyard of one of the houses that made up the sprawling suburbs surrounding the main square.

'What do we do?' one of the men said, sounding panicked. 'We can't fight that thing. We don't have any anti-armour weaponry.'

Raven somersaulted off the roof of the house behind them and landed just a couple of metres from the startled soldiers, a glowing katana in each hand.

'That's the least of your worries,' she said with a nasty smile.

In the church tower Franz watched the purple blades slashing away for a few seconds before he lowered his binoculars, looking distinctly pale.

'You know,' he said to himself, 'I am really wishing that I hadn't been watching that.'

Amidst the chaos unfolding in the streets below Franz did not notice a figure dressed in black hurrying across the square, dashing from cover to cover, heading for the church doors.

Inside the tank, Wing wrenched on the controls and sent the tank smashing straight through a brightly coloured, timber-clad house as he continued his pursuit of the fleeing remnants of the Disciple forces.

'Fire!' Otto yelled and Shelby pulled the trigger. The shell struck the rear of one of the abandoned military trucks that had been parked in the middle of the road ahead of the

Disciples troops and it flipped up into the air before slamming back down on the road in a cloud of smoke and fire.

'OK, forget the Ferrari,' Shelby shouted, a massive grin on her face. 'The day I get my driving licence, I'm getting one of these things.'

'I'm not sure they're that easy to buy second-hand, Shel,' Otto yelled back, 'but, yeah, I do know what you mean.'

Back inside the church, Tom and Laura levelled their rifles at the door at the far end of the aisle as the handle slowly turned. A woman with a veiled face, dressed all in black, walked into the church.

'Don't move!' Tom yelled at the woman. 'You take one more step and we shoot.'

'Oh, you don't want to shoot me, young man,' Minerva said. 'You see, the organisation I represent would not take kindly to anything happening to me. They might hurt all sorts of people if that were to happen. They might even be people that you care for, isn't that right, Miss Brand?'

'Drop the gun, Tom,' Laura said, turning and pointing her rifle at his head. 'I don't want to kill you but I will if I have to.'

'Laura,' Nigel gasped, 'what on earth are you doing?'

'The only thing I can. Now drop the gun.'

Otto aimed the tank's cannon at the handful of remaining Disciple troops as they backed up against the cavern wall. There was nowhere for them to run. Suddenly Franz's voice crackled in his earpiece.

'Otto, come in, Otto,' Franz said urgently.

'What is it, Franz,' Otto replied.

'There is someone who is wanting to be speaking to you,' Franz said, sounding frightened.

'What do you mean, what's going on, Franz?' Otto asked.

'Hello, Mr Malpense,' a dry, rasping voice said in his ear. 'My name is Minerva and I would very much like you to surrender immediately to my troops. If you don't I'm going to execute all of your friends who were hiding in the church one by one while you listen. Do not make the mistake of thinking this is a negotiation. I expect to see you shortly.'

The line went dead. Otto sat there for a moment, his mind racing, trying to formulate some kind of plan but he realised there was nothing he could do. Whoever this Minerva was, she suddenly held all the cards.

'Guys,' Otto said, suddenly feeling a sense of creeping despair, 'they've captured the others. We have to give ourselves up.'

☻☻☻

The Disciple commander shoved Otto roughly in the back, pushing him towards the centre of the square where his friends were already kneeling in a line with their hands on their heads.

'Ahhh, Mr Malpense, so good of you to join us,' Minerva said as the commander forced him down on to his knees.

'What happened?' Otto said, looking at Tom.

'Why don't you ask her?' Tom said bitterly, nodding towards Laura, who was standing nearby, staring at the ground.

'What are you talking about?' Otto asked, genuinely confused. 'Laura, what's he talking about?'

'Tell him, Miss Brand,' Minerva said. 'Tell him what a fool he's been. Tell him how you were the one that gave us the location of the Hunt. Tell him how you tricked him into obtaining that information for us. Tell him everything.'

'Laura,' Otto said pleadingly, 'what's she saying? That can't be . . .'

Otto fell silent as he realised that this was exactly what he had already begun to suspect. That someone within their group had betrayed them. But it couldn't be Laura, it just couldn't. No matter how he tried to deny it, deep inside he knew that it was true. He thought back to Laura persuading him that hacking into H.I.V.E.mind would be fun and how she'd been so relieved that he'd managed to discover the location of the Hunt when she'd thought they'd lost everything. But more than that he knew it was true because he could feel his heart breaking.

'I'm sorry,' Laura sobbed, still staring at the floor. 'I had no choice.'

'You had no choice?' Otto shouted, suddenly angry. 'What do you mean, you had no choice?'

'They have my family!' Laura shouted back at him, her voice filled with anger and despair. 'My mum, my dad, the baby brother that thanks to H.I.V.E. I never even knew I had! I MEAN I HAD NO BLOODY CHOICE! They were going to kill them.' She began to cry, tears rolling down her face. 'They were going to kill them all unless I did exactly what they told me.'

'Oh God, Laura,' Shelby said, tears in her eyes too. 'Oh hon, please tell me you didn't do this.'

'But I did, Shel. This is all my fault,' Laura sobbed. 'All those people died because of me. I had no idea what they were planning. If I'd known, maybe I wouldn't have . . . I dunno . . . maybe I'd have been able to stop all this. Now I don't think I can live with all this blood on my hands.'

'Laura,' Otto said, 'look at me.'

Laura looked at him, her bright green eyes red with tears.

'This isn't your fault, you didn't kill anyone . . . they did.' Otto pointed at Minerva. 'And I promise you, no matter what, we're going to make them pay for every last drop of blood they've spilled.'

'Such optimism, Mr Malpense,' Minerva said coldly, 'but I fear that the only way you are going to have your revenge on me is if you come back and haunt me and I'm afraid I don't believe in ghosts. Don't worry though I'm not going to kill all of your friends. Miss Brand has earned a reprieve with her exemplary service and young Mr Darkdoom is worth far more to me alive than dead. These two,' Minerva gestured towards Tom and Penny, 'I don't know these two. It seems they had nothing to do with the destruction of Overlord so I am minded to spare them. Especially when they are such promising candidates.'

'Candidates?' Tom asked. 'Candidates for what?'

'Oh, you'll see, my dear,' Minerva hissed, 'you'll see.' She motioned to the commander of the Disciple forces. 'Take these four to the transport.'

'Yes, ma'am,' the commander replied, hauling Laura to her feet. She twisted out of his grip and ran to Otto, hugging him.

'It was Dekker,' Laura whispered in his ear. 'Dekker works for the Disciples. I love you.' The soldier pulled her off Otto and dragged her away at gunpoint. Another two soldiers lifted Nigel on to a stretcher. Tom and Penny followed along behind with their own armed escort.

'I know you're here,' Minerva suddenly shouted to the air. 'I know you're watching, Raven. Surrender now or I put a bullet in his skull.' She pulled a pistol from inside her coat and levelled it at Otto's head. 'You have five seconds. One . . . two . . . three . . .'

Otto felt his heart sink as he saw Raven step out from the shadows of one of the buildings destroyed by their tank. She walked towards them, her hands raised in the air.

'Far enough,' Minerva said. 'Lose the weapons.'

Raven slipped out of her tactical harness and let it drop to the ground. One of the Disciple soldiers ran over and picked it up as two more kept her covered with their rifles.

'Hands behind your back,' Minerva instructed. 'Commander, tie her hands.' The commander walked forward and pulled a thick cable tie from one of the pouches on his belt. He looped it round Raven's wrists and pulled it tight with a zipping sound.

'You couldn't let them die, could you,' Minerva said, walking towards Raven. 'Sentimentality was always your weakness, Natalya.'

'Who are you?' Raven asked, her expression furious. There was something hauntingly familiar about the woman's rasping voice.

'Don't you recognise your handiwork, my dear?' Minerva said, lifting up her veil. The hideously disfigured face beneath was covered in scar tissue, the relics of what must have been horrific burns. Despite the disfigurement there was one thing that had not changed – her eyes. Eyes that Raven would never, *could* never forget. In that instant Otto saw something in Raven's expression that he had never seen before. Fear.

'That can't be. You're dead . . . I watched you die,' Raven gasped, her eyes wide with horror.

'No, Natalya,' Anastasia Furan said, 'you didn't kill me, you just left me wishing you had. You betrayed me, you killed my brother Pietor and you helped that brat destroy Overlord. For that I am going to make you watch me kill these children with your own weapon.' She put her pistol back into the shoulder holster inside her coat and took one of Raven's katanas from the soldier that had been carrying them. 'Then I'm going to use it on you.'

Anastasia walked towards Otto, Wing, Shelby and Franz.

'I'll even let you decide which one goes first,' she said with a sadistic smile.

'Just get on with it, you scar-faced old hag,' Otto said, his voice filled with contempt, 'or are you going to try to talk us to death like Overlord did. I honestly can't tell you what was better – the fact that Overlord died in agony or that he was wearing your brother's body like a cheap suit at the time. I suppose you'd call it two birds with one stone.'

Anastasia turned towards him, her face furious.

'You obviously have a death wish, Mr Malpense,' she snarled. 'Well, consider your wish granted.'

She raised the sword above her head. Otto closed his eyes. The world seemed to slow as he used every ounce of his mental strength to push past the electromagnetic shielding that Professor Pike had installed round the tiny but incredibly powerful fuel cell that powered the sword's variable geometry forcefield. He could not see but could sense the sword swinging towards his neck in slow motion as he commanded the fuel cell to discharge all the power it contained in an instant. The handle of the sword detonated like a tiny bomb with a bright white flash. Furan shrieked as the blade clattered to the ground, clutching at the shredded remains of her hand. The soldiers nearby staggered backwards rubbing their eyes, temporarily blinded by the light of the detonation. Otto opened his eyes and leapt forward, slamming into her and knocking her off her feet. They tumbled backwards together as Otto reached inside her coat and pulled the pistol from her shoulder holster and pressed it to her forehead.

'Drop your weapons, all of you,' Otto shouted to the Disciple troops, 'or I pull the trigger.'

'Shoot him!' Anastasia hissed. 'That's an order.' Otto cocked the hammer on the pistol, pushing the muzzle harder into her scarred brow.

The soldiers looked to their commander, unsure what to do. The commander raised his rifle, aiming it at Otto. In the split second before he could pull the trigger there was an enormous explosion above them. Everyone's heads snapped upwards just in time to see the blazing wreckage of the Disciples' helicopter gunship crash into the glass dome overhead. The dome disintegrated as the doomed aircraft hit it and the blazing remains of the helicopter and a shower of giant glass shards plummeted towards the startled occupants of the square below.

'Run!' Otto yelled at his friends as the Disciple troops scattered in all directions. Otto leapt to his feet and sprinted for cover in the fire station garage as Anastasia Furan staggered to her feet and ran in the opposite direction. The commander of the Disciple troops seemed frozen in place as the burning hull of the gunship fell from the sky and smashed down on top of him. The explosion knocked Otto and his friends off their feet, sending them sprawling. Massive glass sheets smashed down around them, exploding in sprays of deadly crystal shrapnel. Otto, Wing, Franz and Shelby all ran headlong for the fire station garage. They dashed inside as more and more glass tumbled into the square, huge sheets impacting like mortar shells. After a minute or so the dust in the square began to settle and the full extent of the damage became visible. The flaming debris of the gunship lay surrounded by tons of shattered glass and the church building was on fire, the flames spreading rapidly across its wooden structure. Several of the remaining Disciple troops had not made it to cover and lay where they had been cut down by the lethal rain of glass.

'Stay down,' Otto whispered to the others as he saw Disciple troops starting to cautiously emerge from the buildings they had taken cover inside around the square. One of them pointed over to the fire station. Otto was just about to shout to his friends to run when the air behind the advancing Disciple troops shimmered and one of H.I.V.E.'s assault Shrouds decloaked. The soldiers never even knew what hit them as the Gatling cannon under the chin of the dropship spun up and opened fire. Seconds later a dozen men in black body armour leapt from the loading ramp at the rear of the Shroud and spread out, forming a defensive perimeter.

'Looks like the cavalry's here,' Otto said with a relieved sigh. 'Guys, this is going to sound weird but don't tell them anything about what Laura did. Let me handle it.'

He looked at his friends, seeing his own confusion, anger and sadness reflected in their eyes. One by one they nodded their agreement.

'OK, let's go.'

Otto, Wing, Shelby and Franz walked slowly out of the fire station and a couple of the G.L.O.V.E. troops spotted them and raised their rifles.

'Hey, same team!' Shelby yelled.

'Hold your fire,' Colonel Francisco bellowed as he ran down the Shroud's loading ramp.

'I think I can honestly say that this is being the first time I have ever been happy to be seeing Colonel Francisco,' Franz said quietly, a relieved smile on his face.

'I'm glad to see that at least some of you made it,' the Colonel said. 'Sorry it took us so long to get here. If it hadn't been for that beacon, I doubt we would have ever found you.'

'Well, you can thank Raven for that,' Otto said, suddenly frowning. 'Hold on, where is she?'

☘ ☘ ☘

Anastasia Furan ran along the corridor leading out of the hidden facility, trying to ignore the agonising pain from her shredded right hand. She had endured far, far worse before now. She reached the shattered exterior doors and stepped out into the daylight. The transport helicopter was waiting, its rotors spinning at full speed, ready for take off. She hurried across the snow-covered ground as the rear ramp of the helicopter lowered and climbed inside with the help of two of the Disciple soldiers on-board. Laura, Tom and Penny sat huddled at the other end of the compartment with Nigel lying on the stretcher next to them.

'Get us out of here,' she yelled at the pilot who pulled on the collective control and sent the giant twin-rotored chopper climbing into the sky. Anastasia looked out of the rear hatch and felt a chill as she saw a familiar figure sprinting across the snow towards the slowly climbing helicopter.

'We need more altitude,' she yelled.

On the ground Raven aimed her grappler at the rear of the transport which was now twenty metres off the ground and fired. The dart attached to the helicopter's metal skin and Raven hit the retraction control, sending herself shooting into the sky, trailing behind the helicopter as it tipped forward and swooped away from the mountain.

One of the Disciple troops on the helicopter braced himself just inside the open hatch, drew his pistol and aimed at Raven as she whipped around on the end of the monofilament line a dozen metres behind the helicopter. The motors in the grappler screeched in protest as they tried slowly to pull Raven towards the back of the transport, fighting against the massive turbulence that tossed her around like a fish struggling at the end of a line. The soldier fired and missed twice before Furan snatched the gun from him with her good hand. She didn't aim at Raven – instead she took careful aim at the silver dart embedded in the helicopter's fuselage just outside the hatch. She fired and the bullet struck the dart with a spark, dislodging it and sending Raven tumbling away into the sky. Furan ran to the rear hatch and looked down at the dark green treetops that flew past below. She handed the pistol back to the soldier and hit the switch to close the rear hatch.

'Goodbye, Natalya,' she said as the hatch closed with a thud.

'We've finished our sweep, sir,' the G.L.O.V.E. soldier reported. 'There's no sign of anyone else inside the facility. The Shroud even performed a thermal scan of the cavern from the air and there's nothing.'

'Understood, lieutenant,' Francisco said. 'Get the rest of your men back on-board the Shroud. We're heading back to H.I.V.E.'

Francisco walked up the ramp to the Shroud's interior and watched as the medic finished checking over the four Alphas.

'They all seem fine,' the medic said as Francisco approached. 'A little dehydrated and some cuts and bruises but nothing serious.'

Francisco nodded and walked over to where the four exhausted-looking Alphas were sitting.

'There's still no sign of Raven or the other missing students,' Francisco said. 'I'm taking you back to H.I.V.E. Nero's orders.'

'We're just going to leave?' Otto said angrily. 'How do we know that the Disciples aren't holed up somewhere nearby with Laura and the others?'

'We don't have time for a full search of the area and Disciple reinforcements might arrive at any moment,' the Colonel said, shaking his head. 'We have to get out of here.'

Shelby suddenly burst into tears, her shoulders shaking as she sobbed. Wing put his arms around her and hugged her.

'We will find them,' Wing said. 'I swear to you.'

The last of the G.L.O.V.E. troops filed on to the Shroud and Francisco headed towards the rear. He walked down the ramp and looked around the debris-filled town square. The fires started by the destruction of the gunship that they'd shot down were spreading and there was little they could do to stop them. Soon the whole facility would be ablaze. He was just about to head back up the ramp when he saw a familiar figure walking slowly towards him across the square.

'You weren't going to leave without me, were you?' Raven asked, raising an eyebrow. She was walking with a slight limp and her bodysuit was torn in several places, blood covering her face from a nasty gash in her hairline.

'You look like hell,' Francisco said, smiling.

'We'll see how you look after you fall from a helicopter,' Raven said. 'The other Alphas are gone. I tried to stop them being taken but I was too late.'

'Nero's ordered us back to H.I.V.E.,' Francisco said.

'Good, I need to speak to him. Our situation may be worse than we thought,' Raven said, frowning.

'What's happened?'

'Let's just say that a ghost from mine and Max's past has come back to haunt us.'

Raven walked up the ramp and into the Shroud, Francisco just behind her. The Colonel closed the loading ramp and the Shroud's turbine engines roared into life, lifting it into the air and up through the shattered remains of the glass dome overhead. As it climbed out of the cavern its cloaking systems engaged. It shimmered for a moment in the fading autumn light and then vanished.

chapter twelve

'How you doing?' Shelby asked Otto as she sat down next to him. They had been in flight for more than an hour and he had barely said a word to anyone.

'I feel like an idiot,' Otto said, staring at the deck. 'How could I have not seen what was happening?'

'Come on,' Shelby whispered, shaking her head. 'There was no way that any of us could have known what Laura was being forced to do.'

'I don't know why she didn't just tell us.'

'Because she was frightened,' Shelby replied, taking Otto's hand. 'She couldn't do anything that might endanger her parents and her baby brother. If she'd told us or even Nero, how could she know that the Disciples wouldn't find out.'

'Oh, I'm pretty sure that they'd have found out,' Otto said with a sigh. He had told no one about Laura's final words to him. There was only one person he was going to give that information to and he was going to deliver the message in person.

☢ ☢ ☢

Dr Nero watched as the assault Shroud touched down on the crater landing pad. The loading ramp whirred into place and Otto, Wing, Shelby and Franz walked down it, closely followed by Raven.

'Welcome back,' Nero said. 'I am truly sorry that you have all had to endure such an ordeal. Rest assured that the people involved will suffer for what they have done. Our retaliation will be swift and decisive. I will also not give up on all of the students who have been captured by these people. I cannot tell you how long it might take but I can tell you that we will not rest until they are returned.'

'Doctor Nero, I need to speak to you in private,' Otto said. 'It's extremely important.'

'Of course,' Nero replied with a slight frown. 'Please wait outside my office, Mr Malpense, I shall be there shortly. The rest of you should return to your quarters and get some rest. I think it's fair to say that you've earned it.'

'What do you need to see Nero about?' Shelby whispered as the four of them climbed the stairs leading up from the landing pad.

'I need to tell him about Laura,' Otto replied.

'I thought we weren't going to tell anyone,' Shelby said.

'I have to,' Otto said firmly, 'because it's the only way he'll believe what else I'm going to tell him.'

'Which is?' Wing asked.

'I promise I'll fill you in later,' Otto replied. 'I know what I'm doing, trust me.'

Back in the hangar Nero walked over to a quiet corner with Raven.

'You said on the radio that there was something we needed to talk about,' Nero said, 'though I still don't understand why you couldn't have just told me then.'

'Too many ears open nearby on-board the Shroud,' Raven explained. 'Max, I know who's running the Disciples. I met her a few hours ago in Siberia, or, to be more precise, I met her *again*.'

'What is it, Natalya?' Nero asked with a frown, noticing her worried expression. 'Who is she?'

'Anastasia Furan,' Raven said, looking Nero straight in the eye. 'She's alive.'

'But that's not possible,' Nero replied, his eyes widening in shock. 'We both saw her die, Natalya.'

'She survived. God only knows how but somehow she survived.'

'As if this situation wasn't bad enough already,' Nero said, shaking his head.

'I want to go after her, Max,' Raven said. 'This is unfinished business and I intend to be the one to finish it.'

'I understand how you feel, Natalya, you know I feel the same way,' Nero said, 'but this is no longer an isolated skirmish between G.L.O.V.E. and the Disciples. This situation has escalated and we need to consider our next move carefully. I need you here for now. There is a war to be fought and you are one of G.L.O.V.E.'s most powerful weapons. I promise you that when the time comes, when the axe drops on Anastasia Furan, you will be her executioner but for now I cannot afford to lose you to a personally motivated mission of revenge. Do you understand?'

'Yes,' Raven said with a nod, 'but, you are right, this is personal for me, in ways that you cannot even begin to imagine. I cannot . . . I *will* not wait for ever. I want blood, her blood, and I want it soon.'

She turned and walked away. Under other circumstances he might have felt a vague sense of pity for anyone that Raven hated with such a passion but Anastasia Furan was someone he too would never be able to feel anything but hatred for. She had murdered the one woman that he had ever truly loved and for that he could never forgive her.

The helicopter touched down on the ice sheet with a bump, its twin rotors slowing as the rear boarding ramp descended. A pair of Disciple soldiers shoved Laura, Tom and Penny down the ramp. The icy wind cut through even the insulation of their environmental suits, their exposed hands and faces stinging with the cold. They trudged towards a concrete block, shrouded in ice with a heavy metal slab set into it. As they approached the slab slowly rumbled down into the ice to reveal a steel-lined lift carriage beyond. They were followed into the elevator by Anastasia Furan and two more Disciple troops who were carrying Nigel's stretcher. Once they were all inside, a set of internal doors closed and the lift began to descend. After a minute or so the lift stopped and the internal doors slid open once again. Suddenly they were hit by the noise of hundreds of voices as they walked out on to a concrete walkway that ran all the way round the outside of the massive circular chamber in front of them. A man in a white coat ran up to Nigel's stretcher and began to examine him.

'We need to get him to medical immediately,' the man said.

'Will he survive?' Anastasia asked.

'I don't know,' the medic replied. 'It looks like he's bleeding internally. We'll do our best.'

'See that you do,' she replied with a frown. 'This boy is strategically valuable and he's no use to me dead.'

'You need to get that hand looked at too,' the doctor said.

'I am quite aware of that, doctor,' she snapped.

As Anastasia and the doctor talked, Laura walked forward and peered over the waist-high concrete wall and down into the vast chamber below. The drop to the large open area at the bottom must have been at least a hundred metres and down there, far below, she could see tiny figures running assault courses and sparring. Every floor of the structure was ringed by an identical walkway, all lined with doors and regularly patrolled by armed guards. Hanging from the centre of the ceiling above them was a multi-storey glass structure that was occupied by what looked like a high-tech control centre. From where Laura was standing the whole place looked very much like a prison.

'What is this place?' Tom asked as he and Penny looked down into the pit.

'This is the Glasshouse,' Anastasia said with a cold smile, 'the most sophisticated operative training facility on Earth and also your new home. Here you will be honed into weapons, those of you that are strong enough at least. Those who are weak, those who fail, will perish, as they should.' She turned towards the waiting soldiers. 'Guards, take the girl with the leg wound to the medical centre and escort Miss Brand and the boy to their new accommodations.'

The soldiers stepped forward and grabbed Laura, Tom and Penny and marched them away. Anastasia looked down into the training area of the Glasshouse and found herself thinking about the previous facility that had gone by that name. She thought of the flames consuming the building around her and unconsciously she reached up and touched the scars that covered her face. Seeing Raven had brought back many unpleasant memories. Natalya had been both her greatest success and her most disappointing failure. The next time that they met she would be made to pay for everything she had done, that much was certain. This was, after all, just the first stage of a much larger plan and by the time she was finished G.L.O.V.E. would lie in ruins and the world would be hers for the taking.

Several floors below a guard shoved Laura in the back, pushing her inside a tiny, cramped cell with a toilet, a sink and a thin mattress on a concrete slab.

'Get changed into these,' the guard said, pointing to the boots, grey combat trousers and white T-shirt that lay on the bed inside the cell. 'I'll be back in five minutes to take whatever clothes you're wearing now for disposal.'

The door to the cell slammed shut and locked with a click. Laura slowly stripped out of her Alpha jumpsuit and put on her new uniform. When she had changed, she sat down on the bed and picked up her H.I.V.E. uniform, staring at the silver fist and globe badge on the chest. As she looked at the badge she began to cry, feeling for all the world like she might never stop.

☹ ☹ ☹

'Now what was it that you wanted to discuss, Mr Malpense,' Nero said as he sat down behind the desk in his office. He gestured to the seat on the other side of the desk.

'No, thank you, I'd rather stand,' Otto said. 'I need to talk to you about how the Disciples discovered the location of the Hunt.'

'We have been investigating precisely that in your absence,' Nero replied. 'It appears that Cole Harrington may have been working for the Disciples and that after he stole the information from H.I.V.E.mind he transmitted it to them. We subsequently found a hidden covert transmitter in his quarters but before we could question him any further about what he had done he took his own life.'

'There's only one problem with that story,' Otto said with a frown.

'And what might that be?'

'It's complete rubbish,' Otto replied calmly. 'Harrington never transmitted that information. He never even saw the location of the Hunt. He didn't even steal the data from H.I.V.E.mind.'

'Then who did?'

'I did,' Otto replied. 'I stole H.I.V.E.mind's source code but only because a core dump was the only way to get a copy of the examination papers. We were all tired of the hard time that we were getting from Chief Dekker and Laura suggested that we get our own back on her by stealing the examination papers. We knew that she had been placed in charge of security for the exams and we figured that getting the questions and giving them to everyone would make her look stupid.'

'I see,' Nero said. 'Go on.'

'Well, I managed to get my hands on the core dump but then Harrington and those two morons, Block and Tackle, jumped us. Before I had a chance to retrieve the exam papers I was forced to use my abilities to copy the data from Laura's Blackbox to Harrington's so that it would look like he was the one who'd stolen the data. I didn't feel too guilty about it considering he was planning to kill us so that he could sell H.I.V.E.mind's source code to the highest bidder. Looking back, I should have realised that there was no way he could have known about the core dump, including H.I.V.E.mind's source code, unless someone had already told him that was what we were planning to do. The same person who had told Laura that if she didn't put this whole plan into motion and get the location of the Hunt for the Disciples, they would murder her family. The person who sent Harrington after us to give her a cover for getting rid of Laura. There was just one thing that they didn't allow for. They didn't realise that H.I.V.E.mind would figure out what was going on and trigger the security alarms. Before they could kill Laura and me, since I was the only witness, the alarms went off and they were forced to act as if they were just reacting to the security alert. At the time I thought that they'd managed to get to the accommodation block incredibly quickly – H.I.V.E.mind had triggered a school-wide alarm, so there was no way anyone could have known exactly where in the school the problem was. Raven only knew where to come because H.I.V.E.mind told her that the door to the accommodation block had been opened. Do you remember who it was that opened the door? Who got there before anyone else? The person who put this entire plan into motion and then presumably killed Cole Harrington to cover her tracks.'

'Dekker,' Nero whispered.

'Bingo,' Otto replied. 'Laura told us that she had been dragged into Dekker's office just before she came up with the plan to hack into H.I.V.E.mind. I'm willing to bet that it was then that Dekker showed Laura evidence that the Disciples had her family and told her that if she didn't do exactly as she was told that they would be killed. Dekker's run this whole thing. We stole the data, Laura gave the data to Dekker, Dekker sent the information to the Disciples.'

Nero pushed a button on his desk. A moment later Raven's voice came over the speaker.

'Raven here.'

'Could you come to my office immediately please – there is something that we need to urgently discuss.'

Nero looked at Otto, his expression furious.

'Do you realise what your actions have caused?' Nero asked. 'An entire year's Alpha students, bar six, missing or dead. A massacre! You must realise how serious the punishment for everyone involved with this will be.'

'Yes,' Otto replied, 'but neither Laura nor I knew what was being planned. If we'd known, even for a second, what was going to happen, of course we would never have done this.'

'Who exactly was involved with the theft of H.I.V.E.mind's source code?' Nero asked angrily.

'Just me and Laura,' Otto lied. 'It was a hack, a very clever hack, but we were the only ones involved. That was why Dekker and the Disciples choose Laura – she's the best hacker in the school. If anyone was going to be able to somehow hack into H.I.V.E.mind's central core it was her. They also knew she was vulnerable, because they knew she had family.'

The door to Nero's office hissed open and Raven walked into the room.

'What's going on?' Raven asked with a frown.

Nero quickly explained to Raven everything that Otto had just told him.

'So how long do you want me to make it last before I let Dekker die?' Raven asked angrily when Nero had finished.

'She doesn't die before I know absolutely everything she does about the Disciples,' Nero replied.

'Understood,' Raven replied.

'There is something else I wish to discuss with you,' Nero said. 'There is the small matter of Mr Malpense's punishment for his involvement in this situation. I fear that I have only one option even when your past service to this school and G.L.O.V.E. is taken into consideration, Otto. There is, however, something you may do to make amends in some way for the chaos that your actions have caused. Here is what I propose . . .'

☺☺☺

Otto walked into accommodation block seven and saw Wing, Shelby and Franz waiting for him on their usual hang-out sofa. He didn't quite know how he was going to tell them what Nero had just decided.

'Hey,' Shelby said, 'how's it going?'

'I've told Nero about Laura,' Otto said, sitting down, 'and I've told him that Laura and I were the only ones involved with the raid on H.I.V.E.mind.'

'It is not right that you should shoulder the blame for that alone, my friend,' Wing said, frowning. 'I would rather we had all taken our share of the responsibility.'

'Wing is right. We are all being involved, Otto,' Franz said, nodding.

'Yeah, stand together, fall together and all that stuff,' Shelby said.

'It's a nice idea, guys, and I appreciate the sentiment,' Otto said with a sad smile, 'but I don't think there's much point in us all getting expelled.'

'What do you mean?' Wing asked, sounding shocked.

'I've been expelled,' Otto said, looking down at the floor. 'I'm leaving immediately. I just came to say goodbye.'

'Oh God, no, Otto,' Shelby said, 'that's not fair. You didn't know what was going on. It wasn't like we helped the Disciples deliberately. It wasn't even as if Laura had any choice. What was she supposed to do – just let them kill her entire family?'

'Don't worry,' Otto said. 'I get the feeling that the person who really caused all this is about to have a really, really bad day.' He explained quickly to his friends about Dekker's involvement in the whole affair.

'I always knew there was something funny about that witch,' Shelby said angrily.

'Yeah, well, Raven's been sent to ask her a few questions so I think it's safe to say that she's going to get what she deserves,' Otto said. 'Look, I haven't got long. I just wanted to tell you all not to worry about me, I'll be fine. This isn't the end. I'll see you guys again. It's a pretty small world for people like us.' He stood up and looked around the accommodation block. 'You know, I never thought that I'd say this but I'm going to miss this place.'

'Come here,' Shelby said, wrapping her arms around him and hugging him hard. 'Who on earth am I going to squabble with now? Take care of yourself, Otto.' She stepped back, her hand to her mouth and tears in her eyes.

'Be having good luck, Otto,' Franz said, shaking his hand. 'You have been a good friend, I will be hoping to see you again soon.'

'Me too, Franz,' Otto said with a smile.

Wing stepped forward and put his hands on Otto's shoulders. 'You are not just my friend,' Wing said, 'you are my brother.' He pulled Otto towards him and hugged him so hard that Otto was afraid he might break his spine. 'And brothers are always together in spirit. Nothing can change that.'

'Feeling's mutual, big guy,' Otto replied, 'feeling's mutual.' He pulled away from Wing and gave the three of them a broad smile. 'Gotta go, Shroud's waiting.' He turned and walked towards the exit without looking back.

'Otto, Laura, Nigel, the whole of our year of Alphas, all gone,' Shelby said, fighting back tears as she watched him go. 'What are we going to do, guys?'

'What we always do,' Wing said, taking her hand. 'Survive.'

☺☺☺

'Hello, Max, what can I do for you?' Diabolus Darkdoom said.

'Diabolus,' Nero replied, 'I'm afraid I have to give you some very bad news. Nigel has been captured by the Disciples.'

'What?' Darkdoom said, looking stunned. 'Where is he? Was he hurt?'

'He was shot, Diabolus,' Nero said sadly. 'His current condition will, I'm afraid, depend very much on how quickly he received medical treatment. Diabolus, there's something else you should know. He was captured by Anastasia Furan.'

'That's not possible,' Darkdoom said, shaking his head, 'Anastasia is d—'

'That was precisely my reaction as well,' Nero sighed. 'Raven was face to face with her – there is no doubt it was her. It appears that she is now at the head of the Disciples.'

'Do you have any idea where Nigel is being held?'

'No, I'm afraid not but I do have an idea how we might be able to find out.'

'Really? How?' Darkdoom asked.

'I'll brief you later,' Nero replied. 'I'm just putting things in motion at the moment.'

'How did this happen?' Darkdoom asked, sounding bewildered.

'The Hunt was ambushed by Disciple forces after its location was leaked to them by Chief Dekker.'

'I don't believe it,' Darkdoom gasped. 'Dekker worked for me for nearly fifteen years. I trusted her completely, that's why I recommended her to you.'

'Raven is questioning her, Diabolus, but the evidence we have so far appears damning.'

'Good God, Max,' Diabolus said, shaking his head, 'she could have been feeding them information for years for all we know. She knew everything about my organisation.'

'It might help to explain how the Disciples got their hands on the thermoptic camouflage technology. Their forces were using it when they ambushed the Hunt.'

'This is a disaster, Max,' Darkdoom said, looking suddenly tired. 'What can I do to help?'

'Just one thing,' Nero replied.

☻☻☻

'Wake up, Dekker,' Raven whispered in her ear as she cracked a tiny stimulant capsule under her nose.

Dekker woke up with a start, struggling against the straps that held her to the chair she was sitting in. She saw Raven standing in front of her with a nasty smile on her face. Without hesitation she crunched her back teeth down hard on the hidden compartment in one of her molars. She closed her eyes again and waited. A few seconds later she opened her eyes as she realised nothing was happening.

'Looking for this?' Raven asked, holding up the tiny capsule that she had removed from Dekker's mouth while she slept. 'Oh, you don't get off that easily, Dekker. Now why don't you tell me everything there is to know about the Disciples.'

'Go to hell,' Dekker snarled.

'You know, I was actually hoping that would be your response. OK, girls,' Raven said, pulling the twin blades from the sheaths on her back, 'looks like we've got a long night ahead of us.'

������

Otto walked across the hangar bay towards the waiting Shroud with a backpack slung over his shoulder. Nero stood beside the loading ramp.

'You have everything you need?' Nero asked as Otto approached.

'Yes,' Otto replied, 'as long as you're sure that the school doesn't need what you've given me more than I do right now.'

'Professor Pike assures me that we will be fine,' Nero replied. 'Be careful out there, Otto. It's more dangerous than you might imagine at the moment.'

'Don't worry,' Otto said with a smile. 'I'm sure I'll find someone to watch my back.'

Nero stuck out his hand and Otto shook it.

'The school will not be the same without you, Mr Malpense.'

Otto nodded and walked up the ramp. Nero watched Otto disappear from view as the ramp whirred shut. He walked away as the Shroud's engines increased in volume and the aircraft lifted off the pad and soared upwards and out of the crater, leaving H.I.V.E. behind.

☣ ☣ ☣

Nero gestured for the other members of the G.L.O.V.E. ruling council to be seated as he walked into the conference room.

'Thank you all for making the journey to be here today. I know it's unusual but we have something extremely important to discuss. You are all graduates of this school, in fact, you are all graduates of the Alpha stream specifically. That is, in large part, why I selected you to make up the new ruling council after the events of Zero Hour. It was not a question of trust or loyalty, it was because you were the best. All of you are therefore familiar with the exercise known as the Hunt. You have all taken part in it at some point and you are all familiar with the special place it has in the history of this school. It is my sorry duty to inform you that two days ago the Disciples ambushed those taking part in the Hunt. So far the toll of those dead or missing presumed captured stands at sixteen support staff and thirty-eight Alpha students. Almost the entire year of Alphas has been wiped out.'

There were gasps of shock and dismay from the others round the table.

'When we last met I told you that we had no choice but to wait for the Disciples to make their move. They did. Now the time has come for retribution. I am not talking about punishment or reprisals, I am talking about the wholesale destruction of the Disciples once and for all. We are going to wipe this scum from the face of the Earth. Ladies and gentlemen, make no mistake, as of now we are at war. This is one of the most serious tests of strength that this organisation has ever faced and we will *not* falter in the face of it. We will need to give our fullest support to one another and also call on the support of our allies. With that in mind I have asked a veteran member of this organisation if he would, despite his reluctance, retake his seat on the ruling council. A man whose own son's name is on the roll of the dead and missing after this atrocity. Diabolus.'

'Thank you, Max,' Darkdoom said, his holographic image appearing in the seat at the far end of the table. 'I always swore that I would not return to being a full member of this council but the time has come for all of us to put aside what we want and do what we must. I don't know if my son is alive or dead but I do know one thing. I know that I'm going to make damn sure that the people responsible are going to pay. I don't care what it takes, they *will* be held accountable.'

'Thank you, Diabolus,' Nero said. 'You should all know that this happened because of a leak within H.I.V.E. That leak has now been . . . plugged. The person responsible was someone we trusted, someone who had served G.L.O.V.E. for many years. I do not want to start a witch hunt within our organisation, but at the same time we have to be aware of the possibility that there are other traitors in our midst. Be vigilant.'

Nero punched a button on the console in front of him and a holographic globe appeared, floating in the middle of the table.

'Here is what we are planning for the first wave of attacks . . .'

☺☺☺

Mary and Andrew Brand sat holding each other, as their baby son Douglas slept in his mother's arms. They had no idea how long they'd been kept there in the darkness but it seemed like a long time since the group of armed men had broken into their house and abducted them. They had undergone a long and terrifying journey in the back of the van with bags over their heads before a man in a mask had taken their photograph and then just locked them here in this bare concrete room with a bucket for a toilet and one meal a day. They had no idea why they were there.

There were heavy footsteps outside and they heard the sound of the door unlocking. The lights in the room came on and two men entered wearing black ski masks. They were both carrying pistols.

'Get the kid,' one of the men said. 'Minerva wants him for the Glasshouse.'

'What about them?' the other man asked, waving his pistol at Mary and Andrew.

'We don't need them,' the first man said, cocking the hammer on his pistol. 'They're expend—'

The two men both gasped as glowing purple blades burst simultaneously from the centre of each of their chests. A moment later the blades disappeared again as both men toppled to the floor to reveal a figure standing behind them in a skin-tight black bodysuit and a black mask, a glowing purple sword in each hand.

'My name is Raven,' the figure said. 'I'm a friend of your daughter. We have to go . . . NOW!'

☻☻☻

two weeks later

Otto walked out of the tube station and on to the street. People bustled around him but he was slowly getting used to being back in a big city after the comparatively small community he had been part of at H.I.V.E. What was harder to ignore was the constant hum of all of the digital devices and networks that surrounded him, day and night. He pulled his wallet out of his pocket and looked inside. He was getting low on cash but that wasn't a problem. He walked for a couple of minutes until he found an ATM on a slightly quieter street. He waited as the woman who was using the machine completed her withdrawal before he stepped up and placed his hand on the numeric keypad. He closed his eyes for the briefest of instants and connected to the machine. First he bypassed the security routines inside the rudimentary computer that ran the machine and then he erased the hard drive inside it that was recording the faces of everyone that used it. He waited as the machine counted his money and then took the several hundred pounds it gave him. For Otto, it was like taking candy from a baby. He walked away down the street, stuffing the money into his wallet.

Don't you ever feel like a bully treating those poor machines like that? H.I.V.E.mind said inside his head.

'Oh, come on,' Otto replied, 'it's not like they've got feelings.'

As far as you know.

'What is this? The digital brotherhood or something?' Otto asked with a grin.

You may laugh but then you don't know how close the internet is to becoming self-aware.

'The internet with a personality, now that *is* a scary thought.'

Suddenly the Blackbox in Otto's pocket began to vibrate. He pulled it out and examined the screen.

'Looks like we're on,' Otto said.

I am decrypting the data packet now, H.I.V.E.mind replied. *There appear to be three separate Disciple cells active within the London area at this time. Should I prepare infiltration parameters for review?*

'Yeah, let's see who the first lucky Disciple we're going to pay a visit to is,' Otto said as the information began to flow into his brain.

On a rooftop nearby a figure pulled a black mask over her head and then drew a glowing purple blade from the sheath on her back. Beneath her mask a smile spread across her face as she watched Otto head off down the street.

'Now it's our turn,' Raven said quietly to herself. 'Let's go get 'em, kid.'

She leapt from the rooftop and disappeared into the night.

☻☻☻

fifteen years ago

Natalya ran across the rooftop and sprang into the air, smashing through the skylight and dropping to the tiled

276

floor of the room below. She drew the two swords from her back and waited. Moments later armed guards began to flood into the room. Natalya dropped a cylinder billowing smoke to the floor and exploded into action. She couldn't see the guards through the billowing white fog but she didn't need to. They were slow, clumsy and noisy. She tracked their movements as they stumbled around her and closing her eyes, she danced. Her swords sang as they swept through the air, moving faster and faster, finding their targets flawlessly. The screams of the guards as they fell just drove Natalya to move faster and strike harder. In seconds it was over, the smoke slowly cleared and she stood alone in the centre of the room, surrounded by a dozen bodies. She knew that her target was close now. She sprinted up the nearby staircase and stopped outside the intricately carved wooden doors at the top. She pressed her ear to the wood, listening for any sound from within but she could hear nothing. She slowly turned the handle and eased the door open. In the room beyond there was a single high-backed chair facing a roaring log fire. Natalya walked silently across the floor towards the chair.

'Hello, Natalya,' Anastasia Furan said, getting up out of the chair and turning to face her. 'Or would you prefer Raven?'

'Madame Furan,' Natalya said, sliding the swords into

the crossed sheaths on her back and dropping to one knee, head bowed.

'You have passed your final test, my dear,' Anastasia said, walking towards her. 'This is the moment you have been trained for. Do you feel ready?'

'I want nothing more,' Natalya replied.

'Very well, but before I give you your first mission I want to ask you something.'

'Of course. Anything,' Natalya replied.

'Tell me, Natalya, do you still want to kill me?'

'Very much,' Natalya replied, head still bowed.

'Then why do you not cut me down now, on this very spot?'

'Because it would change nothing,' Natalya replied.

'Would it not give you satisfaction?'

'I feel no satisfaction in killing. I am an instrument, a tool, a weapon. If it is not you wielding that weapon then it will just be someone else. You talked to me many years ago about the illusion of choice. You were right – you have taught me well.'

'Then truly you are ready,' Anastasia said with a smile. She picked up a large manila envelope from the table beside the chair and unsealed it, pulling a black and white photograph from inside.

'This is your target. He murdered someone I loved very much, many years ago. He is an elusive and dangerous man and that is why his execution must be swift and merciless.'

'Of course.'

'His name,' Anastasia said, handing Natalya the photograph, 'is Maximilian Nero.'

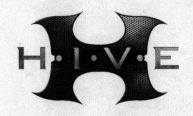

PERSONAL FILE

H·I·V·E

Which Stream are you?

- ALPHA
- HENCHMAN
- TECHNICAL
- POLITICAL / FINANCIAL

Turn over to begin the test . . .

Answer the following questions to find out which stream you belong in.

1. If you were an animal, which of the following would you be?

A. Panther
B. Rhino
C. Spider
D. Snake

2. How might you make one of your enemies sorry?

A. With a hypnotic trigger phrase – so that every time someone says 'Pass the salt', they cluck like a chicken
B. Break every bone in their body – even the ones they didn't know existed
C. Rewire their alarm clock so that it always goes off at 4 a.m.
D. Discover their most embarrassing secret, and publicly expose it – after blackmailing them for a brief, yet lucrative, period

3. If you could choose any instrument to aid you in your villainous cause, what would it be?

A. Nothing – your cunning is all you will ever need
B. A bazooka
C. A computer
D. Money – after all, it is the root of all evil

4. You decide to take over your school. How would you achieve this?

A. Simply inform the headmaster that you are indisputably the most qualified person for the job – you had read every book in the library by the time you were four years old, and have a better understanding of the subjects than the teachers do

B. Threaten to show the headmaster what his/her spleen looks like if control of the school is not relinquished immediately

C. Hack into the computer system and rewrite all of the school's files to show that you are, in fact, already the headmaster

D. Infiltrate the local council and appoint yourself as Head of Education – why settle for just your school?

If your answers are mostly As . . .
Alpha: The Alpha stream specialises in leadership and strategy training. You exhibit certain unique abilities which mark you out as one of the leaders of tomorrow.

If your answers are mostly Bs
Henchman: Your aggression knows no bounds, and you are happiest when you're doing damage to something, or more likely, someone. Your uncluttered, uncomplicated mind makes you the perfect trusted subordinate.

If your answers are mostly Cs
Technical: There's not a computer that you cannot hack, or a bomb you cannot defuse (or build, for that matter). You put the 'EEK!' in computer geek.

If your answers are mostly Ds
Political/Financial: You have a brilliant head for figures (as well as ways to fudge them), and also happen to be excessively charming and a natural born liar – the perfect combination for a successfully sinister career in politics or finance.

Your Stream has been selected. Now take the test to discover how villainous you are ...

1. You find a wallet on the floor filled with ten pound notes, do you:

A. Immediately take the wallet to the police and hand it over, still filled with the money

B. Help yourself to some of the money and then take it to the police

C. Take the money, throw the wallet in the bin and spend the cash on stolen blueprints for the nearest bank

2. You see a small child eating your favourite ice cream, do you:

A. Ask the child where he got the ice cream and set off to buy your own

B. Explain to the child that ice cream is bad for the teeth and make them feel guilty enough to hand it over

C. Organise two henchmen to suspend the small child upside down over a duck pond while you enjoy the icy goodness of their treat

3. Your parents agree to buy you any birthday present you want, do you ask for:

A. Nothing, you would rather your parents treated themselves

B. A new hi-fi and games system so you can lock yourself away in your bedroom

C. A small island in the middle of the Pacific, fully equipped with secret hideout, submarine base and lasers

4. When buying a new house what room is your priority?

A. An ecologically sound conservatory

B. A huge communications room so you can spy on your nearest and dearest

C. An underground lair complete with torture devices and a shark-filled pool

5. You have a red button in front of you that you have been told never to press, do you:

A. Quietly read a book, never giving the button a second thought

B. Stroke the button gently, always feeling tempted to give it a good push

C. Instantly press the button – you built this doomsday device so why shouldn't you use it!

6. An army of robots is about to take over your town, do you:

A. Find a way to foil the robots and destroy them for ever

B. Find a way to foil the robots but keep one just in case you might need it one day

C. Find a way to foil the robots because frankly your army of GIANT SPACE ROBOTS will do a better job

7. You need to hire a henchman, who do you hire:

A. Your mum

B. A couple of ex-cons you found through eBay

C. A suitably subservient weakling who will bow to your every needs . . . and a GIANT SPACE ROBOT

8. You have captured your heroic foe and can at last be rid of him, do you:

A. Have a change of heart, let him go and give yourself up to the authorities

B. Give the hero five minutes to escape from a shrinking room while making a quick getaway

C. Take a long time to explain your convoluted plans for ruling the world, realise the hero has escaped and send your GIANT SPACE ROBOT after him

If your answers are mostly As . . .

To be fair you don't really have a villainous bone in your body. In fact, I suspect you would rather share a cup of tea with your foe, talk about old times and generally have a nice time. It's probably best to give up villainy now and try something more suited to your needs, say knitting or looking after bunnies.

If your answers are mostly Bs . . .

OK, so you have some villainous traits but you're not quite ready for big time yet. You're the kind of villainous soul that would pull only half the legs off a spider so they would have some chance of getting away. With a little training you could be a decent villain but you're no way ready for the big league.

If your answers are mostly Cs . . .

Hello future megalomaniac and ruler of the world. You are a vile villain through and through. You've probably got some plans to take over the world hidden in a draw somewhere and if you haven't already undergone training in Applied Villainy at H.I.V.E. then you should be applying for a place now. Oh, and I hear that GIANT SPACE ROBOTS are currently half-price at your local superstore.

Details of H.I.V.E. students and instructors for your Villainous files

STUDENTS

Otto Malpense
Orphaned at birth, Otto is a criminal genius with a limitless mind, photographic memory and rare extra-sensory skills. Using a robotic mind control device he coerced the British Prime Minister into mooning at a press conference, and ended up in H.I.V.E.

Wing Fanchu
Otto's best friend, Wing was recruited into H.I.V.E. due to his exceptional skill in martial arts and numerous forms of selfdefence.

Laura Brand
Laura has an uncanny expertise with computers, so much so that she made it into H.I.V.E. by hacking into an US military airbase in order to use their military frequency to find out if one of her friends was gossiping about her behind her back.

Shelby Trinity
This all American girl is actually a world renowned jewel thief known as The Wraith. Shelby stole her way into H.I.V.E.

Nigel Darkdoom
It's tough following in your father's footsteps, particularly when you're small and bald and your dad is the infamous criminal mastermind Diabolus Darkdoom. Nigel has a lot to live up to. He does, however, have a talent for science and a strange affinity with plants.

Franz Argentblum
Franz is son and heir to the largest manufacturer of chocolate in Europe. Like Nigel, his father is also a criminal mastermind. Franz is most easily recognised by his impressive size and strong German accent.

Lucy Dexter
The granddaughter of the Contessa (deceased) and has inherited her special talent for mind control.

INSTRUCTORS

Dr Nero
Dr Maximilian Nero is the founder and headmaster of H.I.V.E. He also happens to be one of the most ruthless and devious men alive, and is a senior member of G.L.O.V.E.

Raven
Natalya (a.k.a. Raven) is the most feared assassin in H.I.V.E. She was originally trained in infiltration and counter-intelligence in Russia. She has a long, curved scar that runs down one cheek, although very few people would know as most people she 'encounters' rarely get a chance to make note of their assailant's appearance before they lose consciousness (if they are lucky).

Colonel Francisco
Head of the Tactical Educational department, Colonel Francisco is thought by the students to be one of the toughest teachers at H.I.V.E.

Professor Pike
Head of the Science and Technology department, Professor Pike may appear disorganised and distracted, but appearances are often deceiving. He is one of the original creators of H.I.V.E.mind.

Ms Leon
Currently, her consciousness is trapped in the body of her fluffy white cat (with special thanks to Professor Pike). Tabitha Leon is an expert at infiltration and counter-surveillance. She teaches Stealth and Evasion at H.I.V.E.

H.I.V.E.mind
H.I.V.E.mind is a first generation artificially intelligent entity and the school's omnipresent super-computer. The purpose of H.I.V.E.mind is to serve and ensure the uninterrupted functioning of the school.

**Join the world's most talented villains
for more incredible adventures at H.I.V.E.
It would be criminal not to . . .**

Thirteen-year-old master
criminal Otto Malpense has
been chosen to attend H.I.V.E.,
the top-secret school of Villainy.
But there's one small catch
– he cannot leave until his
training is complete. He's left
with one option. Escape. He
just needs to figure out how.

A new power is rising to challenge
Number One, the most formidable
villain alive. But who is it? And why
do they want to assassinate Otto
Malpense, star pupil of H.I.V.E.,
and his best friend, Wing Fanchu?

H.I.V.E. is in grave danger.
Dr Nero, its leader, has been
captured by the world's most
ruthless security force. It's up
to Otto to save him, but first
he must escape from Nero's
sinister replacement.

One of the world's most powerful villains is threatening global Armageddon, and Otto, Wing and his most trusted villain-friends find themselves in the sights of the most dangerous man alive, with nowhere to run to.

Otto Malpense, star pupil at the top-secret school for Villainy, has gone rogue. In a deadly race against time, Raven and Wing must find Otto before the order to eliminate him can be carried out.

The evil A.I. Overlord is about to put his terrible plans into action. Then no one will be able to stand in his way. It is time to activate Zero Hour, a plan designed to eliminate any villain on the brink of global domination.

Otto Malpense will return. Make sure you're waiting